September Songs

A Love Story

September Songs

A Love Story

Melvyn Chase

SUNSTONE PRESS

SANTA FE

Sunstone books may be purchased for educational, business, or sales promotional use.
For information please write: Special Markets Department, Sunstone Press,
P.O. Box 2321, Santa Fe, New Mexico 87504-2321.

Book and Cover design › Vicki Ahl
Body typeface › Bell MT
Printed on acid-free paper

———————————————————————————

Library of Congress Cataloging-in-Publication Data

Chase, Melvyn, 1938-
September songs : a love story / by Melvyn Chase.
    p. cm.
ISBN 978-0-86534-851-6 (softcover : alk. paper)
1. Autumn--Fiction. 2. Reminiscing--Fiction. 3. Man-woman relationships--Fiction.
I. Title.
PS3603.H3794S47 2012
813'.6--dc23
                        2012007595

———————————————————————————

WWW.SUNSTONEPRESS.COM
SUNSTONE PRESS / POST OFFICE BOX 2321 / SANTA FE, NM 87504-2321 /USA
(505) 988-4418 / ORDERS ONLY (800) 243-5644 / FAX (505) 988-1025

With love to my grandchildren—
Zachary, Lauren, Nathaniel and Ethan—
For all their todays, and all their tomorrows.

Prologue

Autumn 2005

For me, autumn has always been the best time.

The chill whisper of wind. Redbrown withered leaves floating mutely to earth. Dawn that feels like dusk. Winter's shadow.

The benign foretaste of Death, that mysterious woman you've seen but never met. Her smug, enigmatic smile. Eyes that tell you nothing but hint at distant passions you've never felt, dark hungers you've only imagined. You've seen what she can do. She's dangerous. And you can be sure you'll meet her someday.

In autumn, it's easier to be my age—sixty-six—because the whole world is feeling its age. But even when I was young, autumn was my favorite. Friends yearned for spring and summer. When I told them I loved the fall, they thought I wasn't serious, that I was trying to be different. I told them I didn't have to try.

This morning, an autumn morning, I took a walk in Sherwood Island Park. The water of Long Island Sound, restless, green, almost gray, lapping the Westport Connecticut shore. The sky crowded with darkbellied clouds, riding a sullen leafheavy breeze. The sun, weak and wizened, keeping a low profile. The autumn trees, halfnaked, shivering, ready to hibernate. A couple of other walkers, two or three runners, a few bikers.

Twenty years from now, when everything I've learned and felt and believed has disappeared with me, the sun, the Sound, the clouds, the trees will still be here. They don't learn or feel or believe. But they'll still be here.

A couple of months ago, astronomers saw what none had seen before: the earliest stages of a supernova explosion, the birth of a star's death. A telescope on a manmade satellite happened to focus on the right place at the right time. When they made the announcement, they looked star-struck, eyes glowing, proud, humble, like a thirteen-year-old boy after a wet dream.

One astronomer said, "Given the distance of that star and the speed of light, what we saw a few days ago happened more than 80 million years ago."

When the light from that simmering explosion started toward us, the dinosaurs were still throwing their weight around. On that scale, you and I just arrived at the party.

So why am I worried about my paltry eighty years, if I live that long? My life? Not even a sandgrain on the beach. But, hey, it's my sandgrain.

1

The Sailor's Castle

A May morning more than a year ago at The Sailor's Castle, a Southport bookstore owned by my friend Morty Gold.

I'd brought bagels and cream cheese. I do that two, three times a week. Morty has an electric coffeemaker in the store.

Morty said, I got a letter from Barbara yesterday.

He read me the letter while we ate breakfast.

Dear Dad,

You should have seen the sunset yesterday. Perfect.

I sat on a wide, flat shelf of rock high above the beach. A family of seals was playing tag in the choppy, white-crowned surf. Two pensive seagulls (brothers? sisters? husband and wife?) sat beside me, gazing across the Pacific, past the horizon, dreaming of a five thousand mile flight to Japan—hitchhiking on air currents, soaring on updrafts and downdrafts, spearing fish dinners on the fly, following the sun to a new home in a quiet Japanese garden.

Well, maybe that wasn't their dream, but it was mine.

Jeff and Niki and I are fine. She's walking now, tentatively, stiff-legged, arms outstretched for balance, like a monster in a horror movie. A very pretty monster.

We hope you'll be able to come out soon and stay with us for as long as you like. You should get to know your granddaughter. There's nothing like changing diapers to break the ice. Say yes. Please.

I look at Niki and imagine her future, all the good things her life can be. But every life has sadness, too. I hope she doesn't have too many disappointments.

And now that I measure my life by hers, it suddenly seems that time is in too much of a hurry. That frightens me.

Think of a butterfly's life. Just a few days. Do their lives matter less because of that? For the butterfly, those days are forever. What if we travel to Mars or some other planet, and we meet creatures who live for ten thousand years? Then we'll be the butterflies, and they'll wonder what it feels like to live and die so quickly.

Jeff's book is going well. How do I know? He has that zombie glaze over his eyes, his Dawn of the Dead look. He spends most of his time with his fictitious friends. He only pretends to be interested in his wife and daughter. Hell, I don't blame him: make-believe people are a lot easier to cope with than real ones.

As for me, I'm getting plenty of work. I do it in fits and starts, when Niki is napping, or at night after we put her to sleep. I guess they like my designs. They keep coming back for more.

Be well, Dad. We love you. We hope to see you soon.

Barbara

"Why don't you go out there, Morty? She keeps asking you. She means it."

He stroked his beard, a thoughtful gesture that he tends to overplay. I have a beard, too, not as full as Morty's—I wear it closely trimmed—but just as gray. And I don't play with it.

"I've gone a few times. You know that."

"So what's the problem?"

"There's no problem."

"It isn't this ridiculous store, is it? You may as well give the books away for nothing, considering what you make here."

"It isn't this ridiculous store, which I happen to love anyway."

"So what's the problem?"

He sipped his coffee, shrugged. He's not a big man and he seemed to become even smaller, his narrow shoulders sagging, his head tilting forward as if his eyeglasses had suddenly become too heavy.

"I love Barbara. And Jeff is a decent guy. I wish she hadn't named the baby Nicole."

"She's only a baby. She isn't your Nicole."

"Of course not."

He was sitting behind the counter. I sat across from him, perched on a stool. He looked down at the framed photograph that faced him. I couldn't see it but I had seen it a hundred times before. His wife, Nicole, who had died fifteen years ago, not yet forty-five. I never met her. Morty and I had only known each other for a couple of years.

I repeated, She isn't your Nicole.

"But Barbara is. Nicole would talk just the way Barbara does. They look at the world through the same eyes. They see things. In a flower, a smile. Seagulls that dream about flying to Japan. I don't understand that stuff."

"Neither do I."

"Barbara's letters make me feel lonelier. Older."

"You are old."

"Not as old as you, you bastard!"

When Nicole died much too soon, Morty made a melodramatic romance-novel decision: he would never love another woman. He stuck to it.

Maybe if she had lived, he would have become disillusioned with her, grown apart from her, even hated her. We all change. But he had frozen his love in time, preserved it. And he was safe now. He would never again lose the woman he loved.

That's one way to survive.

"I saw the poster in the window. You finally got Buddy D'Amico for a Jazz Night? How'd you manage that?"

"He's not doing me any favors. He's on tour, publicizing a new book and a CD that goes along with it. It's called *A Riff for Rosie*. Rosie's his wife. His third wife. So he's willing to come in with his trio, play a couple of numbers, sell some books, make a little money. He can practically walk here from his house."

"You'll get a good crowd."

"He's been around forever. When he was starting out, he played with Chet Baker and Gerry Mulligan."

"I had an LP of a live concert they did in San Francisco in the Sixties. Pacific Jazz. Nice funky music."

"An LP, he says? LPs are ancient history. God, you're an old fart."

I laughed. "It's next Monday, right? I'll help you set up."

"Thanks, old man."

Morty finished his bagel, asked, "How's your book going? I don't hear you talking about it. Not a good sign."

"I'm nowhere. Lots of empty words. I'll let it rest for a while before I take another shot."

"You'd better not waste time. You're running out of it fast."

I nodded toward one of the shelves near the counter and said, "You know why I keep coming back here? It isn't because I care about you, that's for sure. It's because this is the only bookstore in America—in the world—in the universe—that still has both of my books on display. Have you sold any lately?"

"No, but we live in hope."

"Not me. I live in Fairfield."

2

Gloria Monday

Monday night. Jazz Night at The Sailor's Castle. Starting time: 7 pm. I was there at 5:30.

Morty had cleared a space for the musicians. Buddy and his sidemen had set up their instruments and sound system late that afternoon.

Morty and I rolled display cases out of the way. Unfolded a couple of dozen folding chairs.

The store had been the ground floor of Morty's house when he and his wife lived there. And later, too, after she died, when their son and daughter were growing up. When the kids left, he converted the ground floor into The Sailor's Castle and moved upstairs.

At a few minutes after six the first Jazz Night guest arrived. A tall, slim redhead, with a sprinkling of freckles. In her forties. Handsome face. Pleasant smile. Stylish slacks and blouse.

She looked at me. "Mr. Gold?"

I pointed at Morty.

She extended her hand to him.

"Hi. I'm Gloria Mundy. I called you last week."

Morty shook her hand.

"Yes. You wanted to arrange a reading. A book signing."

"That's right."

"I sell a lot of your books." He turned to me and explained, "Women's issues."

Gloria added, "Lesbian issues, too."

I said, "Why didn't I think of that? Maybe I would have sold a few more books."

"Ms. Mundy—"

"Gloria."

"Gloria. This is David Berger, my friend. An author, too."

"With a difference. If I had to live on my royalties, I would starve to death. Morty scheduled a reading for both of my books. Nobody showed up at either one of them. Except for a young woman who asked me to direct her to the cook books. Fortunately, I knew where they were."

"It's a tough game."

"The good news is, my books are still on sale here."

"I'll buy them before I leave."

"Now I can afford to spend the summer in Paris."

Gloria studied me for a moment. Sized me up.

"You're wondering why only two books at my advanced age?"

"Is that what I was wondering?"

"I didn't start writing fiction until after I retired."

"From what?"

"Writing speeches. I was the corporate dramatist. Every speech, a soliloquy. Hamlet in the boardroom. Macbeth with stock options."

"Have you ever written about that?"

"No."

"You should."

I felt a little embarrassed by the reproachful look she gave me.

She said to Morty, "My new book is coming out in a few weeks. It's called *Lady Be Good—To Yourself.* It's about how well women get along without men."

"Another best seller for sure," I said.

Morty nodded. "I read your interview in *Publishers Weekly.* Good stuff. We can talk later, if you're willing to stick around for a while."

"I'm not in a hurry. I'm a native now. A Southporter, if that's what you call it. I just bought a house on Pequot Avenue. Moved in last week."

I wondered, "The one that looks like a cottage in Provence?" (I had seen the *For Sale* sign.)

"That's a nice way to describe it."

"I used to imagine living in that house."

"In Provence?"

"In Southport."

"Why didn't you buy it?"

"There were always too many things going on. It was never the right time."

"I have no kids. Maybe I'll leave it to you in my will."

"Now all I have to do is outlive you."

Other Jazz Night guests had joined us.

Morty said, "We've gotta schmooze a little. I'll see you after the show."

Buddy D'Amico, his wife Rosie, his drummer and pianist (are those electronic gadgets still called "pianos"?) didn't show up until almost 6:45. By that time, all the chairs were filled and there were a dozen people (including me) standing on the perimeter of the room.

Buddy looked like a middle-aged accountant, short, slender, thick eyeglasses. Everyone applauded when they saw him. His wife was in her twenties, clearly proud to be the wife of.

"Thank you, thank you."

He stepped behind his vibraphone, picked up the mallets, two in each hand, introduced the drummer, a stocky, pony-tailed thirty-something: "On the drums, Mr. Rhythm, Billy Wilcox."

Scattering of applause.

"On the keyboard," (a very young man, hovering over his instrument like a lioness protecting her cubs) "the magical fingers of Rob Randall."

He bowed in the direction of his wife. "And of course, the lady I celebrate tonight and every night. My wife. Rosie."

Some people applauded.

"Now here's *A Riff for Rosie.*"

He traced a quick, jagged beat in the air with the mallets in his right hand. The drummer stroked his cymbals with brushes, picking up the beat and turning it into sound. After a few bars, the keyboard reinforced the rhythm, weaving a lacy counterpoint to it. Buddy slipped in with a trace of melody, stepped out, then back again with the full tune, rich, velvety, syncopated.

He coiled and uncoiled, swayed, crouched. The mallets raced from note to note, chord to chord. He didn't look like an accountant any more.

The audience swayed with him.

What was it like to have so much talent? To be the best at something? I'd never known that feeling. Never would.

I wasn't envious. Just sorry I wasn't special. And used to the idea.

I looked around the room. Gloria Mundy was seated a few feet away. I could see her in profile. A fine profile. She sat very straight, foot tapping to the beat, hands folded in her lap. A little too restrained for jazz.

She was living in the house of my dreams. I wasn't. So what else was new?

She turned, looked at me. I tried to read her expression but couldn't. She looked away.

Gloria Mundy.

Today was Monday, wasn't it? Gloria Monday.

Giving her a new name made me feel better. It was as if I had invented her.

Gloria Monday, I created you. I made you up. You're a success, you're beautiful, you're living in my dream house because that's the way I wrote the story. But don't get too comfortable. I may decide to knock you off your high horse. I can do that any time I please. Nothing is forever.

Sic transit Gloria Monday.

3

A Literary Luncheon in Provence

One evening at the end of that week Gloria Monday called. She said she had read both of my books.

That's a rare achievement, I said.

Why didn't I come to her place for lunch tomorrow, so we could talk about life, literature and the pursuit of happiness? (That's not what she said, but it was implied.)

Saturday afternoon. At her cottage, which should have been in Provence, Gloria and I drank Pinot Noir and feasted on Roquefort, Camembert and pâté, crusty French bread and apple slices.

We sat in a screened-in sun porch facing a cozy tree-shaded garden. A cool breeze—*le mistral?*—freshened the air with the scent of spring flowers. My books lay on the table between us.

She asked if the house lived up to my dreams.

It did. But I said, Nothing ever does.

"That's the feeling I get from your stories."

"If I had started writing sooner, when I was young. . ."

"Could be."

"You don't think so?"

"That isn't fair. I'm probably misjudging what you do. I don't write fiction. I have a lousy imagination. I'm a lowly nuts and bolts writer."

"How to be a happy lesbian."

She laughed. "That pretty well sums it up."

She crunched an apple slice, thought a moment, said, "All of your characters—almost all of them—are lonely. Even your love stories are about loneliness."

"I guess so."

She picked up *Souvenir*, my first book, a collection of short stories.

"I like the premise—stories that are not about love, but about the memory of love."

She opened the book carefully, as if the pages were fragile.

"The poem at the beginning. Kind of tepid. And a downer."

I already felt threatened. I knew the poem wasn't very good. Oh, what the hell.

"I wrote it a long time ago."

"How long?"

"When I was in college."

"You must have been a gloomy kid."

"Like you said, That pretty well sums it up."

She read aloud:

> *"Souvenir*
>
> *"The children don't believe me*
> *"When I say I used to sing,*
> *"And throw a ball, and wander free.*
> *"It taxes their imagining*
> *"That I, who dully watch them pass,*
> *"Once loved you, year by day by hour,*
> *"Once kissed you in the tallest grass.*
> *"I should have saved a flower."*

I defended myself. "You know, Thomas Mann was only thirty when he wrote *Death in Venice*."

"But he was German. He had to keep putting verbs at the end of the sentence. That would depress anyone."

She laughed at her own joke.

"I like the dialogue," she said. "You don't waste words. I like that, too."

"The art of speechwriting. Get to the point fast."

"I really enjoyed three of the stories. I mean, I thought all of them were very readable. But there were three. . ."

"Which three?"

"One was about the guy who's got all this crap in his life—his pain-in-the-ass wife, his miserable kids, his rotten job. But every once in a while, he spaces out and remembers his first love, his sweetheart back in high school."

"And if he had married that girl, she would probably have turned out to be just as big a pain in the ass."

Gloria shook her head.

"That's not what the story says."

"That's why they call it 'fiction'."

She sipped her wine, watched me for a long minute. "I was surprised by *Mrs. Leslie*. It was—sweet."

"I was surprised by it, too."

"You made marriage seem wonderful. Do you have a wonderful marriage?"

"For a while I did. My second marriage. That's over now. My first marriage was nothing to write home about."

She hesitated. Was she feeling a little gun-shy?

"The third story, *Galatea*, was too well done. It made me a little uneasy. No, a lot uneasy."

"Me, too."

"I wish you'd stop agreeing with me. You're making me nervous."

"You don't look nervous."

She leaned toward me.

"When Michael says, 'I've always confused beauty with character,' I know what he means. I've made the same mistake. I keep making it."

"It's what they call 'romance.' You don't meet the woman or man you love. You invent her. A year goes by, or two, or however long it takes. Finally, reality sets in. You're disappointed. She's not what you thought she was."

"And you're not what she thought *you* were?"

"Absolutely. It works both ways."

She put *Souvenir* back on the table, picked up my novel. It was as if she needed a physical connection with a book before she could talk about it.

"I love the title. *The Dancer and the Jackal*. But when I read the blurb, I wasn't encouraged. Italian wars in the fifteenth century? Not exactly my favorite subject."

"But you read it anyway."

She nodded.

"Out of a sense of duty to your fellow author?"

"Actually, your note at the beginning piqued my interest."

The note said, "This isn't a historical novel. I've used history, but also abused it. I've compressed time, allowed myself a few anachronisms, juggled some events. Because it's the story that matters, not the setting. Scholars: please forgive me. Readers: please come along with me."

"I enjoyed it more than I thought I would."

I groaned, Talk about faint praise.

"I didn't mean it that way. But why do you keep avoiding the present tense? Short stories about memory. A novel about the fifteenth century. Even though you claim it's not. You always distance yourself from the people you write about."

"I don't think I'm doing that."

"If I were writing fiction, I would dig into the world around me. My own life. The people I know."

"That's okay up to a point. You have to transform your experience into something more interesting."

She shrugged, raised her eyebrows.

Two or three glasses of wine had weakened my defenses. In fact, I didn't feel threatened any more. I tried to rise to the occasion. To be literary.

"Real life is dull. One day crawls after another. With a couple of special moments once in a while. But basically you keep eating, drinking, sleeping, whatever. Eventually it ends. But there's no 'The End' at the end. It's just over—for you. Other people go on living. Eating, drinking, et cetera. Until it's their turn to end."

"And I thought Thomas Mann was depressing."

"That's why a writer has to shape what happens. It's chaos, but you give it form and direction. So it seems to have some meaning."

She nodded but didn't buy it.

"You're not as cold-blooded as you say you are. You have sympathy for your characters."

"Sure I have sympathy. We're all in this mess together."

She poured more wine for both of us. Took a long sip. Nibbled on a chunk of Roquefort. Didn't say another word for a couple of minutes.

I followed suit.

Then I asked, "Why do you care what I write? You're successful. You run with a much faster crowd. Why are you interested in *me*?"

She thought about that for a minute.

"As I've said, I can't write fiction. I don't have the talent. But I hate to see talent wasted."

"So I guess I'm just your latest project. Is that it?"

"It sounds pretty cold when you say it that way. And besides, I like you."

"I don't mind being a project. As long as I know it. And I like you, too."

I asked her one more question: "Am I obligated now to read your books?"

"Not unless you want to be a happy lesbian."

"Who would want to be an *un*happy lesbian?"

She drank some more. Chewed some more. Maintained her silence again.

The wine soothed me, relaxed me. The breeze brushed my face with its airy fingers.

I was enjoying my literary luncheon in Provence with Gloria Monday. Watching her. Watching her watch me.

"Are you writing anything now?" she asked.

"Struggling. Not really getting anywhere."

"A novel?"

"Yes."

"What's the setting? Ancient Greece?"

"Vienna in 1914."

"You're all the way up to the First World War, huh?"

She smiled and there was a peculiar seductiveness about that smile, although it wasn't sexual. It was more like a dare.

"David, why not try something closer to home? Closer to yourself?"

"I was really looking forward to trench warfare. Poison gas. All that good stuff."

She said she was serious.

"I know. Maybe you're right. Maybe that's why I'm not getting anywhere."

"Could be."

"I'll think about it."

"Good."

I became the silent one for a couple of minutes. Drinking. Chewing.

Then I said, I was lying before. This house, her house, did live up to my dreams. It was beautiful.

"Are we going to be friends?" she asked.

"I think so."

"So do I."

"What have I got to lose?"

She smiled a comfortable smile.

"More wine?"

4

The Art of War

I don't see my son Philip very often. That suits both of us.

I barely know his kids, my only grandchildren. But they get plenty of attention from Philip's in-laws, Marie's parents. He works for Marie's father, in one of those accounting firms that cook the books for the *Fortune 500*.

I used to think accounting was a science. Until I started writing news releases about corporate earnings. Then I realized that, like most things, it was only a game. *Generally Accepted Accounting Principles?* Three Card Monte.

Apparently, Philip plays the game pretty well. And it doesn't hurt to marry the boss's daughter. They have a Better-Homes-and-Gardens house in Greenwich. Not a mansion on Lake Avenue. Not yet. But he's only thirty-two.

As I said, we don't see much of each other. But he always invites me and Mandy, his mother, to his birthday parties. She and I catch up on Philip's latest achievements. Make very small talk with his wife and extremely dull mother- and father-in-law. Remind his children that they have two sets of grandparents. We're the ones that *send* them their presents (although they're too young to care). And say very little to each other. So there's more than enough awkwardness to go around.

When I drove up to Philip's house late in the afternoon, two other cars were already parked in the circular driveway. At least I was consistent: I was always the last one to arrive. And, of course, I was wearing my arty writer's outfit—brown corduroy sports jacket with leather elbow patches, khaki chinos, beat-up loafers. You get the picture.

Marie greeted me at the door with a humorless smile and a dry kiss. She was a pretty woman, but quite unattractive. Her eyes were flat and empty, as if she were blind and only pretending to see.

She ushered me into the living room, which was overlarge and overfurnished, but not overcrowded. Philip's birthday celebrations were always limited to his parents and Marie's parents. Son Michael (six years old) and daughter Stacy (four) would be displayed by their nanny after the festivities were well under way.

I shook Philip's hand, said Happy Birthday, and gave him his present, a rare 1885 edition of Machiavelli's *Art of War*. Morty had tracked it down for me.

One thing Philip and I shared was an interest in military history.

I said hello to his in-laws (Hal and Holly—they sound like a 1940's singing duo, don't they?) who were seated on one of the couches. He's lean and aggressive. She's a faded natural blonde with the furtive gaze of an antelope that has just detected the scent of an approaching lion.

Marie didn't ask what I'd like to drink. She handed me a glass of red wine. *Mi casa es mi casa.*

Mandy was standing by the window, half-turned, as if we were merely a distraction.

She was wearing a silky print dress. The line of her body was slim and strong. Even now in her mid-sixties, she moved with the arrogance and energy of youth.

She lives and works in Manhattan, where Philip works. So she meets him for lunch once in a while. Not often.

I kissed her cheek and stood beside her.

"How's it going?" I asked.

"Fine. What about you?"

"Can't complain."

I waited for someone else to say something. No one did.

I turned to Philip and raised my glass.

"If I may. A toast to the man of the hour. The thirty-two-year-old man of the hour. Happy birthday, Philip."

My son was never comfortable at the center of attention. Not as a child. Not as a man. He's tall, several inches over six feet. But he slouches. He has Mandy's thick, dark hair, but wears it close-cropped, almost drill-sergeant style. He's handsome, but doesn't think of himself as handsome. I guess he feels he doesn't deserve to be attractive and smart and successful. Might as well blame that on his parents.

Hal, not to be outdone by me, added his own toast. "Happy birthday to the firm's new junior partner."

We all murmured, Congratulations.

I gave Philip a book for his birthday and Hal gave him a partnership in his company. So I guess we came out about even.

"That's great," Mandy said, with as much sincerity as she could muster.

"That's my boy," Marie said, and smiled. It was no idle boast.

Looking at that icy smile, I felt myself pulling back from the moment, as if I were changing focus on a camera from close-up to long shot. As if I were outside of time, watching my whole life race by in a few seconds. And wondering how it could possibly have turned out this way.

How could I be sixty-six years old and sometimes still feel like a hopeful teenager? How could my son be a stranger to me? How could my wife and I be so far apart? How could our daughter have died so long ago?

I tried to refocus the camera, to slow down time, to listen to the conversation.

". . .a unanimous vote of the partners," Hal was saying.

"Unanimous," Holly echoed, like a back-up singer.

Hal: "He did us proud."

Holly: "Proud."

If you added a few more voices, some funky costumes and a little doo-wop choreography, they could play Las Vegas.

Hal, Holly and the CPAs. Oh, yeah!

Philip sipped his wine, smiled and tried to turn everyone's attention away from himself.

"How are things going with you, Mom?"

Marie, Hal and Holly looked at Mandy as if she had just farted.

"Fine, fine," she said. "These days I'm in the catbird seat. A kind of advisor emeritus. I get involved in the juiciest cases, but the young lawyers do all the grunt work."

"It's only fair," I said. "You were on the receiving end when you were their age."

"But nowadays it's almost impossible for them to become partners. So they resent me even more."

"A little hate is healthy," I said.

25

"What about you, Dad? Working on a new book?"

I nodded, grimacing slightly to suggest the unique anguish of the creative artist.

"What's it about?" Hal asked, with an overt lack of interest. I could see Holly's mouth silently form the word "about".

"At the moment, it's about eighty pages."

An old joke. Mandy laughed. No one else did.

"It must be discouraging to work on your books for such a long time and get so little for your efforts," Marie said.

The silence was deafening.

Marie watched me intently with her lifeless eyes. Hal suppressed a smile. Holly wasn't sure what to do. Philip started to say something but stopped.

I thought of how pleasant it would be to hoist Marie up by her thumbs.

"You know, dear," Mandy said, "we lawyers and accountants don't understand the pleasure that writers or painters or musicians get from what they do. Writing books is an art. Selling them is a business."

"Some people can do both," Marie said.

"Some people can't," I observed. "One does what one can."

I nodded a Thank you to Mandy.

Philip had left the conversation for a moment. He was looking up at a framed photograph on the wall to his left. I'm willing to bet it was the only picture of our family in his house. A relaxed, informal portrait. Mandy and I were fifty-two, fifty-three. Philip and Lisa were teenagers.

Philip loved Lisa as much as we did. He also believed that because of her we had cheated him.

He once told us, "Dying was a brilliant move. That let her off the hook. She could never disappoint you."

"It's time for dinner," Marie said.

"Dinner," Holly said.

5

The Caretaker's Cottage

I live in the caretaker's cottage. That's not a heavily-freighted symbolic statement. It's a fact.

For many years, a wealthy old coot—in the perfume business, I believe (the sweet smell of success?)—lived in a decaying mansion on a dozen acres in Greenfield Hill, the ritziest section of Fairfield. The caretaker's cottage at the edge of the estate was a modest little place on a fenced-in, woody half acre. Two bedrooms, a bathroom, an eat-in kitchen, and a comfortable living room with a brick fireplace.

When the old man finally died, his son and daughter, who were already in their late sixties, launched a ten-year battle of suits and countersuits—a Connecticut version of *Jarndyce vs. Jarndyce*.

By the time the multiple cases were settled, the son had succumbed to a heart attack and the daughter had been institutionalized. She claimed that her father appeared at the foot of her bed every night singing Christmas Carols in German. (He was Jewish.)

The children of these unfortunates sold the estate to a developer, who demolished the crumbling mansion, built two elegant houses in its place and dumped the caretaker's cottage on a speechwriter he knew, who was living alone, separated from his wife.

I didn't want to stay in the Fairfield house where Mandy and I had spent so many years together. I didn't want to waste a lot of time remembering. Anyway, who needs all those rooms?

As the least wealthy person in the neighborhood, I'm performing a valuable community service: everyone else there has someone to look down on.

The cottage decor is Spartan, to say the least. I have little interest in furniture, and no taste, either. The most important room to me is the smaller bedroom I use as an office—computer, fax, filing cabinets and a shelf with *both* of my books on it.

When I came home after Philip's birthday party, I sat at the computer, opened the draft of my new novel and stared at the first page for a long time. I didn't scroll to the second page.

I began to wonder if Philip's party could be a grain of sand in my oyster: an irritant that becomes a pearl. The characters, the crosscurrents, the backstories were all there. Gloria would have said, Go for it.

But I wasn't about to write a confessional novel. For one thing, I didn't have much to confess. I hadn't throbbed my way through a dozen torrid love affairs. Or fought in the Spanish Civil War. Or dwelt as a brooding expatriate on the *Rive Gauche*, romancing Juliet Greco and trading *bon mots* with Camus and Sartre.

No such luck.

I started scrolling through the draft. I wasn't impressed. There were a lot of clever words, well chosen but empty.

The story had no juice. It was too careful, too cautious. The work of someone outside looking in. A caretaker's book.

I left the office, brewed a pot of coffee, poured myself a cup and sat by the fireplace.

I thought of Mandy. She still looked great. And she had defended me from that bitch Marie. But we had said very little to each other. That was par for the course.

I call her now and then, but I'm terrible on the phone. I don't like talking to people when I can't see them. And we really have very little to say to each other. We've already said too much.

Philip seemed so isolated. Even with his children, he didn't warm up.

And when we sang Happy Birthday to Philip, his daughter started to cry because it wasn't *her* birthday cake. I wanted to say to Marie, "That's your girl."

The phone rang. It was Ted Copeland. He and his wife, Elaine, had been friends of ours for more than twenty years. When we separated, Elaine discarded me. Ted tries to keep in touch. But I've never been much good at friendship.

Gloria says my stories are usually about loneliness. She's right and she's wrong. Despite having lots of friends and business acquaintances, marriage, children, the core of me has always been alone. But not really lonely. That is, not unhappy about being alone.

"How's it going, Dave?"

"Good. How's things with you?"

"Well, I'm getting closer to—I can't say it."

"Retirement!"

"It scares the hell out of me."

"Relax. Take the advice of someone older and marginally wiser. You'll get to love it."

"Six months and I'm out the door. When you reach sixty-five at my company, you have no choice."

"They can't make you retire, can they? Aren't there laws against that?"

"It's in my contract."

"I forgot. I was a peon. You're a big shot. An officer and a gentleman."

"Well, you're half right."

"Have you bought that place in Sarasota yet?"

"Just about. We're finalizing everything in a couple of weeks."

"Is Elaine ready?"

"She's felt like quitting her job for a long time."

"Are you staying down there all year?"

"No. When we sell the apartment, we'll look for a smaller one in the city. A couple of rooms. What do they call it: a *pied-à-terre*. So we'll be able to come back to New York whenever we like. You know, the kids are here."

"Makes sense."

"You talk to Amanda lately?"

"As a matter of fact, I saw her today. At Philip's birthday party."

"Is she thinking about retiring soon?"

"I doubt it. She loves her work. Always did."

"Elaine and I had dinner with her a couple of weeks ago. I'll say this for Mandy: She still won't let Elaine badmouth you."

I laughed. "I think your wife was more upset about our separation than mine was."

"Could be."

"Philip's father-in-law just made him a junior partner in the firm."

"No telling how rich your kid is going to be."

"Between him and Mandy, I look like a piker."

"But can they write novels?"

"The question is, can I?"

"You working on a new book?"

"Yes and no. I'm having second thoughts. I might try something else."

There was a long pause. Then Ted said, "At dinner the other night, we were talking about the trip we took to Venice."

"Jesus, that's ages ago."

"Mandy is working on a case involving an Italian software company. She's going over—not to Venice. To Milan. But it reminded her of that trip."

"The good old days?"

"I guess so."

"Remember the first night?" I wondered.

"No, I don't."

"We were at this cafe down by one of the canals. There was a cool breeze blowing. You could smell the salt in it, among other things. Lots of boats floating by—gondolas and ferries packed with people. The sun was setting. It looked like orange fire on the water. We were drinking wine. There was a trio—a couple of guitars and a mandolin—and they were singing love songs."

"Yeah, yeah. I remember."

"If you could hold on to those moments. Keep them safe somewhere."

"You ought to write that stuff down."

"Maybe I will."

"Why don't we get together for lunch soon? Before all the retirement and relocation shit hits the fan."

"Sure. I'll call you at the end of the week and we'll set something up."

"Okay, my friend. *Arrivederci.* Take care of yourself."

"I'd better. Nobody else will."

I refilled my coffee cup and went back to the computer. I clicked onto a clean screen.

I kept thinking about that day in Venice. About other days that I remembered.

Maybe Ted was right. (And Gloria, too.) Maybe I ought to write that stuff down. Maybe that stuff could be my new novel.

Not the actual details of my life. Not my memories. Just the *kind* of memories I wanted to keep safe somewhere.

A story that would have shape. That would make sense.

If I could make sense out of it.

Would I show it to Gloria? Maybe not, if there was too much truth in it. Maybe I wouldn't show it to anyone.

I sat at the keyboard searching for a beginning.

After a couple of hours, I thought I had at least found a voice. And had written a few lines that could survive a second reading.

I turned off the computer and went to bed.

This is what I wrote:

> *If you reach the age of eighty, you will have lived more than 29,000 days. When you look back on your life, the chances are you will have forgotten most of those days.*
>
> *But some of them, the days you remember, are usually the ones that shaped your life. For better or worse.*
>
> *In fact, the days you remember are your life.*
>
> *Let me tell you about the days Daniel Berman remembered.*

6

Mary, Mary Meets the Holy Fairy

On Tuesday night, Gloria called me.

She invited me to the reading of a play written by a friend of hers.

"It's called *Mary, Mary Meets the Holy Fairy*," she said. "Jan Webber— she's the playwright—says it's a take-off on the New Testament."

"I've always thought the New Testament itself was kind of funny."

"To a Jew like you, maybe. But I don't recall many chuckles in church."

"When and where is the reading?"

"Thursday. Eight o'clock. At the Theatre on the Green in Bridgeport. Have you ever been there?"

"A few times. It's small, comfortable. Intimate."

"Okay. You can take me. And let's have dinner first."

"You know what your problem is? You're too shy. Would you like me to mow your lawn before we go to the theatre?"

"I'll let you pick the restaurant."

"There's a pretty good Italian place a block or two from the theatre. My treat. Despite the fact that you're a lot better heeled than me."

"Hey. I just put a codicil in my will: you're inheriting my house. What do you want, blood?"

"Should I know Jan's name? Have any of her plays been produced?"

"At regional theatres. Usually for short runs. Rarely reviewed. Nothing that amounts to much money. It's not a very profitable line of work."

"And even if you make it to the stage, the director or the cast may screw it up."

"A few years ago, one play of hers ran in Greenwich Village for almost a year. In a loft. No scenery. No curtain. A capacity audience of forty. It got a good review in *The Village Voice*."

"I probably won't understand all the gay jokes."

"All you have to do is laugh when everyone else does."

"It sounds like a delightful evening."

"Deal with it. By the way, Friday I'm starting my book tour."

"Where are you going?"

"Four cities. I sell enough books by now to call the shots. San Francisco. Chicago. Boston. And New York. Major bookstores. Some morning TV shows. Dumb questions. Canned answers. It's very tedious. The whole thing'll take about three weeks. And I promised Morty a reading when I come back."

"You're completely ignoring the lesbians in Mississippi? And Montana? Is that fair?"

"My book isn't only for lesbians. It's about getting along without men. You don't have to be a lesbian to dislike men."

"So you're an equal opportunity hater."

"Pick me up at five-thirty."

"Yes, ma'am."

At dinner on Thursday I said, "Do you mind if I ask you: Is Jan a former—what should I call it?"

"How about lover?"

"—a former lover of yours?"

"I don't mind if you ask. Yes, she is. Was."

"And—never mind."

Gloria nodded as if she were answering a question, sipped her *Chianti Classico* (the food hadn't arrived yet), and said, "You want to know more about my sex life."

I raised my hands in a gesture of surrender.

"It's none of my business."

"I'm not shy. If I were shy about sex, I couldn't sell any books."

"True."

She paused, thought for a moment.

"When I was growing up," she began, "like most kids I was very excited about sex. The boy-girl variety."

"Romance."

"Not exactly. For me, even then, even when I was only imagining it, sex was just about pleasure. At first, it was the pleasure men could give me. But I never enjoyed the intimacy before or afterwards. I didn't want a relationship with a man. They aren't worth the trouble."

She watched me, studied me. I didn't react.

"As I got older, I began to meet women who were smart and creative and independent. I admired them. I tried to be like them. And their friendship became more and more important to me. Sometimes that friendship included sex. Pleasure is pleasure. But it was only a byproduct. Now and then I've revisited the boy-girl bit. I'm not straight. I'm not gay. I'm just me."

Again I thought, A little too restrained for jazz.

"That makes sense," I said.

She smiled. "Here comes the pasta."

After several mouthfuls I said, "Sex wasn't easy for me. I was the classic geeky teenager—acne, big nose, skinny. I skipped a grade in junior high, so in high school I was younger than I should have been. And I looked it. I spent a lot of time by myself."

"Alas."

"Sex was a mystery—a romantic mystery. I would see those French New Wave movies, with all those beautiful, pouting women, and dream of being Jean-Paul Belmondo. Charming, suave, irresistible."

"He was cute."

"Well, I never turned into a sexy guy. But even when I caught up and finally solved the mystery, it was the romance of sex that still appealed to me. That beautiful girl across the room. The approach. The discovery."

"And the disappointment?"

"Even the disappointment."

"Confusing beauty with character?"

"You bet."

We ate silently for a few minutes.

"In other news," I said, "I've ditched my First World War novel."

"Too contemporary for you?"

"I'll ignore the sarcasm. I'm taking your advice. Staying closer to home."

"How does it feel?"

"I've barely begun. We'll see how it goes."

"If you want to bounce it off somebody, I'm available."

"Maybe."

She smiled and whispered, "Chicken?"

"No comment."

"You know the old cliché: a tree falling in the forest. If nobody hears it . . ."

"It still makes noise."

"I'll try not to hurt your feelings."

"I'll show it to you if it's any good."

"How will you know if it's good unless you show it to someone. Namely me."

"We'll see."

"Promise me you'll show it to me."

"No. Okay. Maybe."

"What is that: multiple choice?"

"Leave me alone. Eat."

She clucked like a chicken a few times and laughed.

"I need another glass of wine," I said.

There were about forty people, mostly women, at the play reading, scattered throughout the orchestra section of the theatre.

Jan, the playwright, was a slim, tense woman in her fifties. Long silvergray hair pulled back in a tight bun. Soft blue eyes. A quick, absent-minded smile.

She and Gloria embraced, kissed. Gloria introduced me. Jan smiled quickly, saw another friend, darted away.

Gloria made the rounds. She seemed to know everyone in the audience. But when we sat down, we didn't sit with anyone else.

In the single-sheet program, the full title of the play was *Mary, Mary Meets the Holy Fairy, or, A Passion for the Passion*. Not bad, but self-conscious. Arch.

Ditto, the play.

Four actors read, some of them taking two or three roles. The bulk of the dialogue was between the two main characters—Mary Magdalene, a lesbian, frightened and confused about life. And Jesus, the Holy Fairy, gay, proud of it, and self-assured, as only the Son of God can be.

There were a few laughs:

Jesus describes Peter by holding his hands two feet apart and saying: "He's my rock."

And when Pontius Pilate points to Jesus and shouts, "*Ecce homo,*" Jesus asks him, "How did you know?"

But after an hour or so, my attention wandered.

The message of the play? God is a Trinity: the straight, the gay, the bi. They're all part of God's divine plan.

We applauded enthusiastically. The playwright went onstage and sat with the actors. There was an extended question and answer session that surfaced a few minor negatives, but featured several over-the-top tributes. Gloria didn't say a word. Afterwards, she declined Jan's invitation to join her and the cast for drinks.

On the way back to Fairfield, she asked me what I thought of the *Holy Fairy.*

"It seemed very Sixties to me."

"Me, too. Jan's still fighting the old battles."

"My uncle never stopped talking about D-Day. It was the only thing he ever did that mattered."

Gloria nodded. "When I first met her, Jan was brave, aggressive. Beautiful. She wasn't afraid of anyone. I was a kid. I needed someone like her to give me courage. I was crazy about her."

She watched the passing traffic for a moment.

"After we'd make love, she would curl up on the bed like a pink cat. Smoke her Parliament cigarettes. Tell me all about love and life and politics. And I'd put my arms around her and dive into those deep blue eyes and feel so safe. That isn't her any more. Tonight she looked so small. Uneasy. Unsure of herself."

"Time is a bitch. (Is that gay enough for you?)"

Gloria laughed.

"Were you bored tonight, David?"

"A little. But I'm beginning to know you better."

"Do you want to know me better?"

"Yes."

"Will you show me your novel? So I can get to know *you* better?"

"We'll see."

"Yes, we will."

She clucked like a chicken and laughed again.

7

The Silverspoon Baby in San Francisco

Halfway through her book tour, Gloria called me from San Francisco.

She said, "I'm pissed."

"I'm not. Should I be?"

"They take it all for granted."

"Who takes what for granted?"

"We weren't even allowed to vote until nineteen twenty."

"Don't blame me. I wasn't born until nineteen thirty-nine."

"They're doctors, lawyers, engineers. Whatever they want to be."

"Bastards!"

"This isn't funny."

"I'm dead serious."

She took a deep breath, sighed. "Well, maybe it is funny. Granted, I'm not from the Gloria Steinem generation. The ones who really took the heat. All the crap from men. And from tight-assed women, too."

"There were plenty of those."

"Even in my time, we still had a fight on our hands. We never passed the ERA."

"Damn it, we don't want a bunch of women in the army and in the Men's Room!"

"That's always been my wildest dream. To fire a machine gun and piss in a urinal."

"So you admit it."

"But the women I'm meeting—the young ones—they don't know the history. And they don't care. To them, everything is Now."

"Instant music. Instant messaging. Never mind the past."

"When we were young, we wanted to change the world. Women. Blacks. Gays. Lesbians. Everybody."

"Not me. I was never a world-changer."

"You were satisfied with the way things were?"

"Politics didn't matter much to me. Never did. I voted for the good people. Contributed money. I even sang the protest songs, but only because I liked the music. I didn't march. I didn't take drugs, or LSD. Or even smoke joints."

"Never? I don't believe it."

"I wasn't a smoker. I coughed too much when I tried to inhale."

"This is a very, *very* sad story," she whispered, melodramatically.

"My drug of choice was a dry Manhattan. What can I tell you? I was a Fifties guy in the Sixties. A fish in the desert."

"Is that an expression?"

"I was a Cold Warrior. I joined the army when I was twenty to stop the Russians from turning the world red. But afterwards, I had tunnel vision. All I could see was my job. My future. And when I had a family, my family."

"A fish in the desert?"

"I made it up. I'm a writer."

She laughed.

"So, Gloria, is your new book selling like hot cakes?"

"Like hot cakes in the North Pole. I made that up."

"Beautiful. And you're pulling in the big bucks."

"I guess so."

"The money doesn't mean anything to you?"

"It's not that I'm allergic to money. But I was a silverspoon baby."

"Is that a religious ritual of some kind?"

"I was born with a silver spoon in my mouth. My father made a fortune. Put a bundle in trust for me. I've never had to worry about money."

"I've lost all my respect for you."

"You don't mean that, do you?"

"What makes you think I had respect for you in the first place?"

"You're taking all of this much too lightly."

"I'm sixty-six years old. I take everything lightly except my prostate."

"My father never made it to sixty-six. He was fifty-three when he died. Heart attack. Gone in thirty seconds."

"A great way to go."

"Maybe. But he was too young. So was I. Just twenty-three."

"The two of you were *simpatico*."

"He was terrific. Intelligent. Handsome. Charming. You could feel the energy radiating from him. And we were on the same wavelength. I miss him."

"Is your mother still alive?"

"She's hanging on."

"Uh-oh."

"She's not my all-time favorite. I haven't seen her or spoken to her for a long time."

"Did she get married again?"

"No. I could never figure out why the hell my Dad married her."

"Did you ever ask him?"

"Actually, I did."

"What did he say?"

"It seemed like a good idea at the time."

"Sounds familiar."

"Is that why you got married?"

"That depends on which marriage you mean."

"Take your pick. You got divorced twice, right?"

"Officially, I'm still married to Number Two. Just separated."

"For how long?"

"About ten years. But let's not talk about me."

"Let's talk about your writing. Are you working?"

"Yes. But it's none of your business."

"Tell me about it."

"No."

"You can get away with this while I'm on the road. But I shall return."

"I'm looking forward to that."

"So am I." She paused and said "okay" to someone in San Francisco. "My 'handler' is getting nervous. I've got miles to go before she lets me sleep."

"Have fun."

"Fat chance. G'bye."

After I hung up, I sat watching the phone for a few minutes. Thinking about our conversation. Remembering.

Then I began to write:

29,000 Days
A novel by David Berger

Remembering

If you reach the age of eighty, you will have lived more than 29,000 days. When you look back on your life, chances are you will have forgotten most of those days.

But some of them, the days you remember, are usually the ones that shaped your life. For better or worse.

In fact, the days you remember *are* your life.

Let me tell you about the days Daniel Berman remembered.

October 7, 1969
8:30 am—Breakfast with Bernard Baruch

October 7, 1969 wasn't just another Tuesday.

It was Daniel Berman's thirtieth birthday. That didn't sit too well with him. He knew that he was supposed to be mature by now. But he wasn't sure what that meant.

It was also the day his bosses at *aXcess* were meeting with Wall Street for the first time since the company went public a few manic months ago.

As usual, Virgil will confuse them. Eli will charm them. Tyler will reassure them.

And it was the day his wife Ginnie asked him for a divorce.

Nineteen sixty-nine. Another violent, dispiriting, angry year. Bobby and Martin Luther King were dead. By year's end, so were Ike and Jack Kerouac.

The War kept grinding on, killing them killing us killing our spirit. Protests. Sit-ins. Marches. Draft card burning, pot-smoking, LSD. Let's get high. Let's get laid. Let's change the world.

But Daniel wasn't hip. He wasn't a worldchanger. He was still locked into the Fifties, imprinted with the Depression-era fears of his parents: no matter what you have, no matter who you are, you can lose everything, just like *that*. So get a good job. Save your money for a rainy day because, believe me, one of these days it's gonna pour.

He was still a Cold War kid, too young for Korea, too old for Vietnam. Graduating from college when he was twenty. Joining the army a couple of months after graduation. A veteran at twenty-three, for him Vietnam was an ugly Hot War abstraction.

His drug of choice was still a dry Manhattan.

And women, ah women! He was so unhip about women. Still romantic, despite what his marriage had become.

He didn't trust Nixon, the shiftyeyed God of War with a Quaker mother and a National Security Advisor who sounded like a B-movie Nazi villain. But he'd never had a passion for politics.

How about those SuperBowlchampion Jets? How about those World Series bound Mets?

Neil Armstrong's slow, clumsy dance on the moon meant more to him than Jimi Hendrix's slow, sinewy "Star-Spangled Banner" at Woodstock.

What mattered to Daniel was his career. Public relations. Speechwriting. Making money, youknowwhatImean?

Sure, it was a hell of a time, but he wasn't interested in hell.

Let the world take care of itself.

■■■

The *aXcess* breakfast meeting was in a downtown Manhattan hotel at 8:30 am, before the Stock Exchange opened. The company's CFO, Tyler Flint (affectionately known as "SkinFlint"), had invited the usual Wall Street suspects: institutional investors, who run pension funds and mutual funds. And securities analysts, who supposedly know which stocks are hot and which are not.

Daniel's boss, Mitchell Reilly, vice president-Public Affairs/Public Relations, had three or four business reporters at his table. *aXcess* was made to order for the press:

> *NEW YORK—Wall Street is abuzz about aXcess, a five-year-old partnership going public in three weeks. The new company's primary asset is Virgil Prince, the heir to a citrus fortune, who just happens to be a genius, with several breakthrough inventions already to his credit: microelectronic telecommunications components that, he says, will revolutionize the communications business. "Someday soon," Prince predicts, "telephone networks will be faster, smarter, easier to maintain, and cheaper to run, when*

calls—and data—and lots of other stuff—are moved from place to place electronically." That opinion is shared by a host of industry experts, including AT&T's gurus at Bell Labs, who are also hot on the trail of "electronic switching." In fact, Ma Bell wants to adopt Prince but he says, "I'm not a family guy. I'm a loner. A free spirit." All the way to the bank. He's been licensing his components to the Bell System and other phone companies here and abroad. And he keeps dreaming up lots of other applications for those components in computers, home entertainment systems, et. al. You name it: Prince says he's got the electronics you're looking for. Now, mother-henned by a Merrill Lynch syndicate, Prince's company is on the verge of an IPO. He'll be the Chairman of the new corporation. His former partners, Elihu ("Eli") Fowler and Tyler Flint, will be CEO and CFO, respectively. Don't you wish you could get a piece of that action?

Although Daniel had worked with Eli and Tyler on their presentations, he had nothing to do at the meeting except wear his nametag and schmooze with Wall Streeters, always a humbling experience: when they discovered he was in public relations, they treated him like the class clown.

He sat at a table far from the dais, out of the line of fire. He looked forward to Virgil's opening remarks, which would be off the cuff and off the wall.

To his right, a skinny young woman in a black dress and a bleak expression sipped her orange juice and riffled through the *aXcess Profile* Daniel had written—a stop-gap document describing the company. It would be replaced by an Annual Report on the corporation's first birthday.

To his left, an elderly gentleman in a dark three-piece suit nibbled on buttered toast, scanning the scene with a tolerant smile. A bulky, old-fashioned hearing aid protruded from one ear. A Phi Beta Kappa key hung from his gold watchchain. (Daniel was Phi Beta Kappa, Rho of New York, but his key never left the box in his underwear drawer.)

The man glanced at his nametag, said, "Daniel Berman," and extended his hand. "I'm Schulman. The Schulman Fund."

"Nice to meet you, Mr. Schulman."

"What do you do for *aXcess*, Berman?"

"Public relations. I wrote that *Profile*."

Schulman picked up his copy, examined the cover.

He read, "I^3 = *Inspiration x Imagination x Innovation* = *aXcess*. You wrote that, Berman?"

"Yes, sir."

"Is it supposed to mean something?"

Daniel was about to deliver a forkful of home fries to his mouth. The young woman turned to look at him.

Lowering the potato-filled fork he said, "It's just a shorthand way of describing what we do."

"I'm still in the dark." He tapped his hearing aid lightly. "You'll have to speak up," he said, but didn't let Daniel respond. "You've heard of Bernard Baruch?"

Daniel shook his head.

Schulman frowned.

"A self-made stockmarket millionaire," he said. "Advisor to presidents. A Jew. And he wore a hearing aid like this one, so when he tuned somebody out, they knew it. Now what is all this mumbo-jumbo about?"

The young woman leaned toward me attentively, the *Profile* pressed tightly to her breast.

"Our business is based on research. Virgil Prince and his people— the scientists and engineers—they're inspired. They're imaginative."

"And innovative," Schulman whispered, helpfully.

"And that's why we're ahead of the curve," Daniel finished lamely.

Schulman pursed his lips and nodded.

The young woman leaned back, clearly disappointed. She turned her attention to *The Wall Street Journal.*

"How old are you, Berman?"

"Thirty. Today's my birthday."

"Happy birthday."

"Thanks."

"Can I come to the party?"

"I would invite you, but there's not going to be a party."

"Why not?"

"It's no big deal."

"Thirty? That's a big deal all right. It's like a man's second bar mitzvah."

Daniel shrugged (trying to look mature).

Schulman laughed and said, "Where's all that Inspiration when you really need it?" and began to eat his scrambled eggs.

A few minutes later Mitch Reilly climbed onto the dais.

"Good morning, ladies and gentlemen. Welcome to *aXcess Corporation's* first Investor Forum as a publicly owned company. I'm Mitchell Reilly, veepee Public Affairs. Thanks for joining us this morning. We're delighted to see all of you.

"The format is simple: you'll hear brief remarks by our Chairman, Virgil Prince. Our CEO Eli Fowler. And our Chief Financial Officer, Tyler Flint. Then we'll open the floor for questions.

"To begin with, let me introduce the guy we call—with good reason—our resident genius, Virgil Prince."

Virgil. A festival of dissonance. Tall, slim, round-shouldered. Fortyish. Shaggy blonde uncombed hair. Unpressed khaki slacks, tieless yellow dress shirt, brown sport jacket at least one size too big.

Detaching the microphone from its stand and holding it close to his mouth, Virgil began pacing back and forth. He moved and spoke slowly, rhythmically, as if he were following a drumbeat only he could hear.

"'electrons deify one razorblade/into a mountainrange.'"

Schulman tapped his hearing aid: "What did he say?"

"He's quoting from e.e. cummings."

"Cummings?"

"A poet."

Schulman smiled. "His Inspiration, I suppose?"

Daniel nodded.

Virgil paced back and forth silently, then continued.

"Electrons. Those sneaky little bastards are everywhere. We think we know what makes them tick. But *do* they tick? Quantum physics says they can be everywhere and nowhere at the same time. They never stop surprising us. 'all ignorance toboggans into know/and trudges up to ignorance again.' The little bastards."

"Berman, you didn't write this, did you?" Schulman asked.

"No."

Schulman turned a little wheel on his hearing aid, which pinged.

Is he tuning in or tuning out?

"Research is so much fun. You don't really know where the hell you're going, but you get there just the same. It's like exploring a vast new country. You don't have any maps. And there are always surprises over the next horizon. Columbus aimed for the *East* Indies and landed in the *West* Indies instead. The world was bigger and fatter than he thought. So is the world of the electron."

The young woman glared at Virgil as if he had insulted her. Schulman looked at Daniel and smiled benignly.

For the next fifteen minutes, Virgil paced to the beat of his distant drummer, tossing jagged sentences at the audience, making bold promises, predicting extraordinary outcomes, hinting at remarkable, undefined future breakthroughs.

The audience of number crunchers assumed he was brilliant (because everyone said so), tried to understand him, then applauded politely (and gratefully) when he surrendered the microphone and yielded the dais to Eli Fowler.

"Poetry," Schulman said, the way a prude would say, "Pornography."

Daniel tried to reassure him. "Here comes the prose."

Eli. Short, dark-haired, compactly built. Dressed like a banker. Ingratiating style. Constantly scanning the faces around him, testing the waters, feeling the vibes.

He put a speech outline on the dais, which he glanced at occasionally. He didn't need it. As usual, he had internalized the speech.

"My job is to transform Virgil's genius into products that we can manufacture cost-effectively. And sell profitably. We call ourselves *aXcess*: short for advanced experiments in computerized electronic switching systems."

Eli smiled. The audience began to feel comfortable again.

Schulman nodded approvingly. The young woman's expression thawed. She leaned back in her chair with a post-orgasmic sigh.

Daniel enjoyed watching Eli perform, publicly and privately. Much less relaxed than he seemed. Drawing opinions out of others without expressing his own. Teasing or abusive with inferiors. Deferential with Virgil. Condescending with Tyler.

"Virgil and his team are visionaries. We translate that vision into new, powerful, scalable telecommunications components. And the telephone industry is scooping them up as fast as we can create them. Faster." He smiled again. "Because they know what we know: the future of the industry is *electronics.*"

Eli scanned the faces in the crowd. He pointed his index finger at his chest and said, "I'm not Virgil Prince. I'm not a scientist or a poet. But I *am* a dreamer, in a way—a practical dreamer."

Well done, Eli. Humble and arrogant at the same time.

"We know that *aXcess* has a terrific future. Because we're already there. And that's why we're such a great investment. That may not be science or poetry, but I know it's music to your ears."

The rest of Eli's speech was a quick, non-technical survey of *aXcess* products and how they would make the world safe for democracy.

His summary: "The price of *aXcess* shares has been rising steadily since we went public. And from our point of view, we've only just begun. Now here's the man who can provide the facts and figures to back up that claim. Our Chief Financial Officer, Tyler Flint."

Tyler. Square-jawed. Blue-eyed. Close-cropped gray hair. Eli's classmate twenty years ago at Cornell. In love with numbers.

He spoke slowly, thoughtfully, without much fire. But he gave the Street crowd what they wanted: the nitty-gritty stuff to write their reports and make their recommendations. "Return on Equity. Current assets to current debt. Cash flow. Net sales to inventory." All that crap.

During the Q's and A's, the young woman at Daniel's table left without saying goodbye.

Schulman of the Schulman Fund shook his hand, wished him a Happy Birthday and departed.

But happy or not, Daniel knew that his birthday had only just begun.

12 noon—Lunch with Ayn Rand

aXcess headquarters. The entire tenth floor of a glass and steel atrium building on Fifth Avenue, north of 59th Street.

The day they moved in, Eli said, "If things go downhill, we can all join hands and jump into the atrium together."

The slim, sharp-edged *aXcess* logo was painted in gold on the glass double doors at the entrance. A burnished brass version of the logo hung over the receptionist's desk like a high-tech guillotine.

The walls, off-white. The doors, dark wood. The paintings, coldly abstract. The office furniture, sleek, utilitarian.

The northeast section of the floor was still empty. A ghost town in reverse, waiting for new hires when the company expanded.

Daniel checked his in-box. Listened to two unimportant voicemail messages.

Nora Weiss, VP Human Resources, knocked on the open door of his office.

"How'd the meeting go?" she asked.

"Fine. They didn't know what the hell Virgil was talking about, but Eli and Tyler did their usual spiel."

"The less they understand Virgil, the better. That's why he's so impressive."

"Well, at least he wasn't wearing a sweatshirt this time."

Nora laughed. "Actually, he dresses pretty conservatively compared to some of the other *mishuganas* in the Tower."

"A couple of weeks ago, I had a nightmare: I was wearing a green jumpsuit. And I was trapped in the Tower—forever."

"You woke up screaming, of course."

"Of course."

"Poor devil." She started to leave his office, turned, asked, "Do you have lunch plans today? Are you in the mood for Chinese food?"

"I'll take a raincheck. Ginnie is meeting me for lunch."

"I'll forgive you this time," she said playfully and left his office.

Daniel wondered what Ginnie was up to. She had spent the past week—*incommunicado*—at her parents' home in Darien, Connecticut. Not a good sign. But he didn't need omens or oracles to know where their marriage was headed.

He remembered another lunch date, about three years ago. Same woman. Same man. But they were strangers then. Mitch Reilly had just hired a new advertising/marketing director, a first for the company.

"She starts next Monday, but she's coming in this morning unofficially for a chat with me. Take her to lunch," Mitch said. "Get acquainted." He leaned closer and stagewhispered, "She's young, single and rich. Need I say more?"

Daniel had asked Nora, "What was your take on her?"

"I don't like to be crude, Daniel . . ."

"Since when?"

". . . But I get the feeling she doesn't think her shit stinks."

"Maybe it doesn't."

"She's twenty-eight. Single. Lives on the Upper East Side, not far from you. Has a BA in History from Brown. An MBA from the Stern School at NYU. Worked for her father's company for five years."

"Her father's company? Do fathers have companies?"

"Hers does. You've heard of *Bachman's Fine Jewelry*?"

"No. I wear a TIMEX."

"There's a *Bachman's* on Lexington Avenue in the Nineties, and one downtown in Greenwich Village. There are a few others scattered around the country—San Francisco, Chicago. I think there's even one in Paris."

"So she's not working to keep body and soul together."

Nora patted her fleshy, forty-year-old hips, said, "Compared to me, she ain't got no body," and added, "but what can you expect from a rich *shicksa*?"

"Mitch asked me to take her to lunch."

"Better you than me."

"Thanks."

"Listen, my friend. You should probably think about marrying her."

"Everybody's trying to fix me up with her. I'm romantic, Nora. I'm gonna marry for love."

"So you can't love a rich girl?"

"I think I should at least meet her before I make any final commitment."

Nora laughed, waved a good-humored goodbye.

The receptionist called him a couple of minutes before noon: Mitch's meeting with Virginia Bachman had ended. Now it was Daniel's turn.

She looked like an Ayn Rand heroine. Tall, slim, angular, smartly dressed. One hand on her hip, her head tilted up and slightly to one side, as if she were looking down at everyone.

Hi, I'm Dominique Francon. Or is it Dagny Taggart?

Daniel extended his hand, said, "Virginia, I'm Daniel Berman."

Her handshake was assertive.

"Call me Ginnie."

"Ginnie. Nice to meet you."

She looked up at the brass logo and whispered, "*aXcess*," with a trace of mockery in her voice.

"It could be worse. Virgil Prince wanted to call the company *Xcess*. It took us quite a while to get him off that kick."

"Charming," she said. Her mouth smiled. Her eyes didn't.

"I'd like to show you around. Introduce you to some people. Then I can tell you more about the company over lunch. How does that sound?"

"Okay."

The introductions didn't take long.

Hank Schuster, vice president and general counsel, gruff, sour, perpetually worried.

The two lawyers who worked for him. Not as sour, but just as worried.

Nora, who had already met Ginnie. She winked at Daniel behind Ginnie's back.

Nora's executive assistant, Helen, a savvy young woman who actually ran Human Resources.

Steve Lawford, director of marketing, handsome, shallow, friendly, thesunwillcomeouttomorrow.

"I'm looking forward to working with you, Ginnie," he said, as if he meant it.

When they left Steve's office, Ginnie said, "Why don't we save the rest of the tour for next week, when I'm official."

"Okay."

She reached into her handbag, extracted a cigarette, lit it with a gold lighter, took a deep drag and exhaled.

"How about lunch?" she said.

They ate at a French restaurant on East 56th Street. He started with a dry Manhattan. She had a Vodka Martini.

Daniel thought she was attractive. Not really pretty, but striking. Her straight dark hair was cut short. She had a broad face and a mouth too big. But he enjoyed watching her smoke, sucking on that cigarette as if she were coaxing it to ejaculate.

She was confusing. Cold, out of reach, sensual.

She asked, "What do you do in the grand scheme of things?"

"Speechwriting. Marketing brochures. A jack-of-all-trades."

"How long have you been with the company?"

"Three years."

"What did you do before that?"

"I worked for *TV Guide* for a couple of years after I got out of the army. What about you?"

She tilted her head back, sucked on her cigarette and said, "I was a silverspoon baby. Born with a silver spoon in my mouth. That's okay with me. I like silver. I like gold even more. I suppose you'd say I had it easy. I worked for my father's company."

"I wouldn't call that easy. I couldn't work for *my* father."

She smiled appreciatively.

"But I learned all about advertising. The past couple of years I developed every one of our campaigns myself. The copy, the design, even the placement."

"Mitch likes your work. He's a tough audience."

They ordered another drink and lunch.

When their second drinks arrived, he raised his glass. "Here's to the future, Ginnie."

"Now tell me all about *aXcess*."

"You've probably read about us."

"Mitch gave me the standard presentation. The oh-so-exciting world of tomorrow. Starting with electronic telephone networks—whatever the hell that means. Don't worry. I'm smart enough to figure it out once I come on board." She sucked on her cigarette, exhaled a thin smoke cloud, then leaned toward him and almost whispered, softly, intimately, "Now tell me what I have to know to survive."

Her mouth was so close. He could feel her warm, smoky breath on his face. Dark brown eyes. Long lashes.

It was as if she had just asked him to make love to her. But of course, she hadn't.

He looked down at his Manhattan. He thought about diving into it to cool off.

"The company started a few years ago. It's a partnership. These are three guys who don't seem to have much in common—but for some reason, they're friends."

"Prince is the inventor, right?"

"Right. He doesn't care whether *aXcess* makes any money. He has plenty. For him, the company is a playground. And he's the one who decides what games everyone will play."

"They say he's a genius. Is he?"

"I guess so. He keeps coming up with stuff that the telephone companies want. And he says the telephone business is just the beginning. He doesn't do it by himself. He's got a bunch of characters working with him up in White Plains at his lab. We call it The Tower—short for Ivory Tower. You should see these guys. They look like they just stepped off a flying saucer. They walk around waving their arms and talking to themselves. They only comb the front of their hair."

Ginnie laughed.

"They wear jump suits and Bermuda shorts and sweatshirts. But apparently they know what they're doing."

He informed her, amused her, enjoyed watching her smoke, eat and drink. And in the weeks and months that followed, hardly knowing when the game had changed, he pursued her, fell in love with her and married her.

(She worked at aXcess for less than a year, then joined an advertising agency.)

To her parents, Daniel was a Jewish social climber. To his parents, Ginnie was a snobbish *shicksa*.

But after his passion had subsided, when they weren't just lovers any more, when they were husband&wife in the everyday world, deciding whether to have children, where to live, whether to let her father buy them an apartment, it turned out that there wasn't much left between them.

Ginnie knocked on the open door of his office, said, "Happy birthday, Danny," shut the door, sat down, lit up a cigarette and asked, "How did the meeting go this morning?"

"Fine. The stock price is up a buck and change."

"Mission accomplished."

"Yeah."

He still enjoyed watching her perform in public: the cool, arrogant, AynRand armor. He was still attracted to her. Even though he knew how fragile, how fearful she was when he stripped away that armor. And how she resented him because of that.

"We were going to have lunch," she said, "but there's no sense wasting time. Let's get it over with."

"I can tell you've been talking to your father. He's such a sentimental guy."

"I didn't go to Darien for advice. I needed a little distance—a little perspective."

"Did you buy me an expensive birthday present?"

"Danny, I want a divorce."

"You call that a birthday present?"

"It is. For both of us."

She leaned back, looked at him tenderly, smiled.

"You're always trying to change me," she said. "I don't want to change. I don't want to become someone else. And I'm tired of defending myself."

He looked at her smile, the tilt of her head, the long lines of her body, as if he were meeting her for the first time. He knew then that he had invented her. That she was still a stranger to him and always would be.

"Your father will be so pleased," he said.

6:45 pm—Dinner with Franz Kafka

Daniel left work early enough to get a seat on the 5:15 Long Island Railroad train to Merrick.

He had lied to Schulman of the Schulman Fund. There was a birthday party for his thirtieth. At his father's house. What fun!

The closer he got to Merrick, where he had lived until he was twenty, the younger he felt. By the time he arrived, he was a teenager again, awkward, insecure. Like one of those haunted, broken characters in a Kafka story—the eternal son, the eternal victim of God the Father, or father the god.

Welcome home, Daniel.

It was only a 15-minute walk to his father's house. Even if he walked as slowly as he could.

The other guests at the festivities? Daniel's sister Carol, seven years old when he was born. Beautiful, intelligent, unambitious, consumed with men as soon as her hormones kicked in. Men of every size, shape, age, race, condition of servitude. Married, unmarried and everything in between. A constant source of angst to Dad and Mom.

Finally married at twenty-nine to Jon Miller, a handsome, slick salesman (ladies' shoes this year) with a passion for gambling and a talent for losing. He and Carol lived in the downstairs apartment in Dad's house, dependent, grateful, bitter.

Their son, Stephen, at six years old, a precocious, charming kid. Maybe too much like his father.

At the corner of the street where he had lived, Daniel stopped. He could see his father's house from here. A spacious, comfortable colonial on a well-maintained acre of land.

For Daniel, it was a perfectly formed, empty shell, the kind you find on the beach. When you hold it up to your ear, all you can hear is a distant, mournful wind.

There were few cherished memories here. His father in constant conflict with Carol. Angry arguments, never resolved. Her marriage exchanging one irritant for another. Meanwhile Daniel the good boy, quietly doing his duty, barely visible in the war zone.

And through it all, a mother who hovered in the background, nursing grievances or anger or fear that she never expressed. Increasingly deaf when Daniel was a child, she refused to wear a hearing aid. Increasingly withdrawn when Daniel was a teenager, she was unable or unwilling to share her feelings, her pain with him. Was her deafness a metaphor for isolation? His father acquiesced in her withdrawal. Was his kindness a metaphor for resignation? When she died two years ago, it was as if she had never been there.

Dad greeted him at the door. Brisk handshake, pat on the shoulder, Happy thirtieth birthday!

Marvin Berman, a vigorous, successful CPA, first generation American, who had pulled himself up by the bootstraps from Lower-East-Side-of-Manhattan Russian-Jewish immigrant poverty. The Depression. Working his way through school. Supporting a family at the same time.

Admirable, yes. Unless you'd heard the story a thousand times. And how easy you had it, compared to him.

Dad looked over Daniel's shoulder, saw no one, asked, Where's Virginia? (He never called her Ginnie; that would have been affectionate.)

"She's still in Connecticut with her folks."

"Problem?" Dad asked, hopefully.

"I'll tell you about that later."

They went into the living room.

Daniel kissed Carol, shook hands with Jon and exchanged a macho high-five with Stephen, who said, "It's your birthday, Uncle Dan. How old are you?"

"Thirty."

"Great age," Dad said. "When I was thirty, Burt and I started our partnership. We had *bupkas*—but that didn't stop us."

"Great age," Daniel echoed.

"Where's Ginnie?" Carol asked. She and Ginnie got along well, although they had nothing in common. Carol was very open and friendly. She got along well with everyone.

"With her folks."

Dad waved a be-patient-we'll-find-out-about-this-later gesture at Carol. She said, "I made your favorite dinner. Beef stew."

"Great."

"Beer?" Dad asked. "Wine? What's your pleasure?"

My pleasure would be to get the hell out of here, Daniel thought.

"Beer," he said.

Dad served a cold bottle of beer to each of the adults, a Coke to Stephen. They sat in the living room, drank from the bottles, talked.

"How's business?" Jon asked.

"We had our first big meeting with Wall Street today. The stock went up more than a dollar, so we must be doing something right."

"How about that promotion of yours?" Dad said. "Wasn't that supposed to be in the works?"

"They're in no rush to pay me more."

Dad leaned forward and pointed his beer bottle at Daniel.

"I keep telling you. You can't wait for other people to do things for you. You've got to be pushy. Be the squeaky wheel. Threaten to quit. Make some noise. Like somebody once said, 'Nice guys finish last.' I don't know who said that, but he was right."

"Whoever he was, I'm sure he wasn't a nice guy."

Dad didn't know how to interpret Daniel's response, so he ignored it.

"How do you like the first grade?" Daniel asked Stephen.

Stephen shrugged.

"Do you like your teacher?"

"She's fat."

"And jolly?" Daniel said.

Stephen didn't answer him. He didn't even shrug.

"I'm going to be in the Tony Bennett contest at the temple," Jon said. He had a strong tenor voice. He was in the temple choir.

"You do a good Tony Bennett," Daniel said.

Jon nodded confidently and added, "Rabbi Singer knows Tony Bennett. He thinks he might come here and judge the contest himself."

"That would be great!"

Jon smiled and nodded again.

"With your crazy schedules," Carol said, "working all the time—I guess you eat out a lot? Or take in?"

"Yeah, we don't do much cooking."

"We?"

"I can broil a steak. Bake a potato. I even make a pretty good meat loaf. I can cook. You'd be surprised."

"I am surprised," Carol said.

"I lived the bachelor life for a few years. Bachelors eat, too, you know. Yeah, I've been spotted wearing an apron now and then."

"What's a bachelor?" Stephen asked.

"A man who isn't married," Carol said.

"I'm a bachelor!" Stephen said proudly.

Dad smiled at Stephen impatiently. He could wait no longer. He asked, "So what's with Virginia?"

Daniel took a deep breath.

"Things haven't been going well with us."

Dad tried not to look pleased.

Carol sighed.

"We don't seem to be able to fix whatever's broken."

"Two different worlds," Dad said.

"I guess so."

"Are you . . . ?" Carol let the question mark hang in the air between them.

"Yes. We're getting a divorce."

Dad nodded several times, slowly, rhythmically, as if he were praying in the temple. And smiling, as if he were certain that his prayers would be answered.

"That's tough," Jon said. He had begun dating Carol when he was still married to his first wife. He knew how tough divorces could be.

"Her people never liked us," Dad said. "Germans and Jews. Not a good mixture."

"They're not Germans, Dad," Daniel said. "Any more than you're a Russian."

"They're *goyim*, aren't they? Snobs. Too good for us. Your mother didn't trust them. I know that."

Daniel remembered his mother when she met Ginnie's parents. Deaf, uncomprehending, ashamed. She didn't trust them? She didn't trust anyone, not even herself.

"Well, it'll soon be over."

"Thank God you didn't have children," Carol said.

"Yes," Dad agreed. "Thank God."

Carol came over to Daniel, put her arm around his shoulder, kissed him lightly on the forehead.

"I'm sorry, Danny," she said.

"Me, too," Daniel said.

"Listen, this is no time for sadness," Dad said, with conviction. "We have a birthday to celebrate. An important one." He winked at Daniel. "And a new beginning."

"Yes, a new beginning," Carol said.

"What's divorce?" Stephen asked.

Midnight—A Nightcap with Becky Thatcher

It was almost midnight when Daniel got home.

Ginnie had already begun to extract herself from the apartment—some of her clothing, all of her jewelry and cosmetics, had disappeared. Their bed was neatly made, hospital corners, as usual. And as usual these days, he would sleep alone.

He was exhausted. He sat on the bed, fell back and stared up at the ceiling. The whole day raced by, a two-minute business newsreel:

Wooing and Wowing Wall Street! The word is out. *aXcess* is the hottest IPO in town. "Buy *aXcess* now, or you'll hate yourself in the morning," says Bernard Baruch, deaf Jewish advisor to the mighty. "I may be dead, but I can still pick 'em!"

Ad Executrix Lowers the Boom! In a surprise move, Mad Ave media maven Ginnie Berman switched agencies today, saying sayonara to Berman & Berman, and hello to a solo. "All I need is me," quoth Ginnie. We agree.

Birthday Bash Bombs in the 'Burbs! Danny Berman's Big Three-Oh Gala was a suburban stinker. An awful time was had by all. (So why is Danny's father smiling?)

Daniel turned off the projector. He went into the kitchen, got a beer from the refrigerator and checked the telephone answering machine. Three messages for Ginnie, which he skipped. One for him from Amy.

Amelia Robbins (nee Aaronson) was almost the Girl Next Door. She had lived three houses down the block in Merrick. She and Daniel had been friends since kindergarten. Lost touch for a couple of years when she went to Yale and he went to NYU. Reconnected at intersession in their junior year when both were at their parents' homes for a few days. Since then they had become escape valves for each other, in person, by phone, by mail. Bragging, mourning, venting about their love lives, sex lives, careers, you name it. Never dating.

Footnote: When they were ten years old, Daniel had proposed to Amy. Her response: "Give me some time to think about it."

She still hadn't given him her answer. And he had never proposed again.

Her message was: "Hi, Danny. Happy birthday! Now you're as old as I am. Finally! I bought you something special for your thirtieth. Call me whenever you get back from celebrating. *Whenever*. No matter what time it is! Say hi to Ginnie for me."

He dialed her number.

Her "Hello" was quick and sharp. She wasn't asleep.

"I guess I didn't wake you up."

"You know me, Danny. Sleep is never a priority. Hey, Happy Birthday!"

"Thank you, thank you. Honestly, I don't feel a day over twenty-nine."

"I told you when it happened to me: it's a big buildup to nothing."

"But it's been a hell of a day anyway."

She reacted to his tone of voice. "Bad stuff?"

"Well, on the positive side, we knocked them out on Wall Street today."

"But?"

"I had a truly festive birthday party at my father's house."

"Ugh. Father knows best."

"Doesn't he, though?"

"How's Carol?"

"She's fine. When I go back there, it's like being in a bad movie. I can predict everyone's lines, including mine."

"Carol was always very nice to me. She loves you."

"I know. I know."

"So I guess it wasn't a great party. And your father isn't exactly crazy about Ginnie."

"Well, that's the other news flash: my lunch date with Ginnie."

"Ptomaine poisoning for two?"

"You guessed it. She wants a divorce."

"That's no surprise, is it? You've told me how it's been lately."

"But it's a failure. Nobody likes to fail."

"Tell me about it."

"I wasn't angry. Or disappointed. But I felt foolish. I looked at her and she was like a stranger. It was as if I had never met her. Never known her."

"I'm sorry, Danny. I wish you'd had a better birthday."

"I second the motion."

"I've got some bad news of my own."

"I didn't even ask you how you are. Selfish bastard that I am."

"I forgive you. Listen, I broke up with Norm."

"You let the trophy boyfriend slip through your fingers?"

"I did indeed."

"You don't sound heartbroken. Are you?"

"No. I'm fine. In fact, he helped me win a case a couple of days ago."

"I'm listening."

"Last week, I was in court. Defending the plaintiff in one of those tedious cases that I do so well. They hire five experts. We hire five experts. The testimony is highly technical. Completely baffling to the jury. The trick is how you interpret that testimony for the *noodniks* who have to decide the case. And I am a master interpreter, if I may be immodest. That's why they love me at Schwartz, Steiner ampersand Steiner."

"Affectionately known as the Three Shysters."

"My opponent's third expert is on the stand, spouting a lot of technical bullshit. The judge's eyes are glazing over. The jurors look like lost souls on a slow boat to Hell. Two pigeons on the windowsill have died of boredom. Even I was fading fast. I had to do something drastic. So I began to reminisce about my so-called love life. And it suddenly occurred to me that the key to my love life is my first-year French class."

"I took Spanish."

"Let me set the scene. In French, adjectives usually follow the nouns they modify—except for adjectives of size, age, beauty and goodness."

"You don't say. I think I just saw another pigeon buy the farm."

"For example, Age. You don't say *une fille jeune*. It's *une jeune fille*. A young girl."

"Is there a point to this? I'm beginning to lose consciousness."

"Shut up. Who was my first love?"

"Who can remember that far back? You were always falling in love.

And boring me with your latest *amour*. (That's French. Not bad for someone who took Spanish.)"

"I don't mean casual, three-week romances. I mean the real thing."

He thought a moment. She didn't wait for him to answer.

"Mark," she said.

"I remember it well."

"I remember it well, too. All ten inches of it."

"You really know how to hurt a guy. A man of normal proportions, though certainly no slouch."

"Never mind your ego. Mark was big, right?"

"Right."

"*Size.*"

"Why did you ditch him?"

"He was a good guy. Sweet, really. But he was madly in love with his dick. And he wanted every woman in the world to love it, too. It was big, but as far as I was concerned, not big enough to share."

"Somehow, I can't feel sorry for him."

"We're talking about *my* love life. Stick with the program. Okay?"

"Okay."

"After Mark, there was Andy Robbins."

"That's a different story. Marriage is a serious business."

"He was so romantic."

"And he was fifteen years older than you. *Age.*"

"Atta boy!"

"He left you for a younger woman."

"He said that it's young women—very young women—who keep him young."

"You were nuts about him."

"He was so smooth. Cultured."

"Not to mention rich."

"But not gross rich. He bought fine things, not flashy things. Paintings, rare books. He made me feel like a princess."

"You've always been a princess."

"But I exceeded the age limit. So the princess became a commoner again."

"Are we still talking about adjectives?"

"I was hurt. I couldn't believe it."

"But you survived."

"Then, last year, along came Norm. *Beauty*. Perfect face. Perfect body. Charming. Graceful."

"Here's my problem, Doctor Freud. I don't have an inferiority complex. I *am* inferior."

"Unfortunately, even beauty gets boring when there's not much behind it. Norm is like one of those mansions on a movie set: the face of it is beautiful, but only the face is real."

Daniel summed up. "Size. Age. Beauty."

"Right. I'm sitting there in court, listening to an expert babble on about patent infringement, and I realize that the men in my life are actually French adjectives. So I laughed."

"In court?"

"That woke everyone up. Except the pigeons."

"They have a lousy sense of humor anyway. You rarely see them smile."

"The judge said, 'Would you like to share your little joke with us, Ms. Robbins?'"

"I hope you didn't."

"No. I apologized. But I really shook up the lawyer for the plaintiff. He never recovered. He kept thinking I had something up my sleeve. I whipped his ass."

"After this, I, too, may be emotionally scarred for life."

"You'll bounce right back when I tell you what I got you for your birthday."

"An old, beautiful ten-inch dick?"

"A rare—very, very rare—first edition of *The Art of War in the 16th Century*. You see, I am paying attention when you tell me those boring war stories."

"Live and learn."

"A friend of mine who owns a book store tracked it down for me."

"It must have cost you a bundle."

"I can afford it. It's leather bound. Gold leaf on the edge of the pages. It weighs a ton."

"That was very sweet, Amy. It's the kind of thing a princess does."

"For her best friend? Sure."

Daniel looked around his apartment for a moment, trying to remember two years of a marriage that had dissolved into thin air. A stranger who had once been his wife.

He said, "You've tried Size, Age and Beauty. Now maybe it's time for Goodness."

"Maybe."

"I'm going to take you out for dinner tomorrow, and you can give me my birthday present."

"I'll have to check my calendar."

"Screw your calendar, Amy. I want to see you."

"What are you so angry about?"

He hesitated. Spoke more softly. "Let's call it a date."

"Is it a date?"

"Yes, it is."

She paused. "What makes you think you're Goodness?"

"Well, I sure ain't Size, Age or Beauty."

There was a long, long silence.

"Pick me up at my office at six-thirty," she said.

8

Gone to Be a Soldier

For a couple of weeks, I delayed calling Ted Copeland about lunch. I was writing, rewriting, polishing, with very little time out.

A worried Morty Gold, who hadn't seen me or my bagels for several days, phoned, wondering if the Grim Reaper had spirited me away.

No such luck, I said. I'm writing. Sunrise to sunset. A *new* new novel.

"You almost sound happy," Morty said.

"But I've got to take a break. I'll see you tomorrow morning."

"Be still, my foolish heart."

"I've been meaning to ask you, what are the latest sales figures for my books?"

"Give me a minute to add up the numbers. Hmmmm. So far this year, five. Significantly better than last year. We're edging closer to bestseller territory."

"Fuck you, Morty."

"I love you, too, David. And remember: we'll always have Paris."

I was exhausted. My eyes were strained from staring at the computer screen. My neck and shoulders ached from bending over the keyboard for endless hours. And all this for a book that might sell 100 copies if I was lucky.

You may be wondering who would publish a virtually unknown (though incredibly talented) writer like yours truly. The Lyric Press of Scottsdale, Arizona, that's who. A small independent outfit. Morty Gold (God bless him) is an old friend of the owner/publisher/editor-in-chief, Gary Baker. Morty hooked me up with him.

Gary makes his money from non-fiction, greeting cards, and big-volume contracts with the state of Arizona—tourist guides, stuff like that. He says that he publishes fiction (quote) "because I love it."

Needless to say, there's no upfront money. The royalties are generous but, in my case, irrelevant. There's no help with publicity. Gary sends out review copies that disappear into the void. He also ships advance copies to a couple of wholesale distributors and Amazon.com. Otherwise the books are printed on a just-in-time basis as orders come in.

He likes my work. If I sent him my new novel, chances are he would publish it. But I still didn't know if I wanted him—or anyone else—to read it.

I called Ted. We'd meet for lunch in Manhattan the day after tomorrow. He was at his office. He sounded distant. Guarded. Not like Ted.

Just before Goodbye, he said, "David . . ." softly, as if he were about to tell me something that mattered. But he didn't.

Not at all like Ted.

The New Haven Railroad to New York City. Not a rush hour train, of course. Them days are gone forever.

Years of commuting. So many dull hours every week. Building your life around a timetable. Using train time to work, read, sleep. Marching in lockstep with thousands of others. From the suburban Gulag to the Emerald City. (Ain't mixed metaphors grand?)

Come to think of it, The Emerald City is a pretty accurate image: glittery surface, hollow interior. Maybe this is just the rant of someone who spent most of his life in suburban Connecticut. But everything in New York moves too fast for me. New Englanders remember their yesterdays. New Yorkers are quick to forget the past. Even 9/11 didn't change that for long.

New York is always about now. And next week. That still revs up my engine for a while. But I can only take it in small doses.

I met Ted at a pricey East Side steak house. Ted's company virtually subsidized the place: client lunches, private parties, after-work happy hours. Ted was probably the biggest spender, so they treated him royally.

He was already at the best table when I arrived. He was in uniform: serious dark suit, pale blue shirt, slightly energetic tie—just energetic enough to hint that he wasn't the stiff he seemed to be.

He was finishing a Martini and had gestured for a refill. I shook his hand at the end of that gesture, sat down and ordered a dry Manhattan. He was a little edgy.

"Still fretting about retirement?" I wondered.

"I guess . . ."

"You're going to miss your expense account, I suppose. Or is that part of the golden parachute?"

He didn't smile. Didn't answer me. He waited until the waiter had brought us our drinks and left.

"Cheers," he said, as if he were toasting the end of the world.

"You don't seem too cheery."

"Yeah." He studied his Martini for a while. "You know how I got ahead?"

Ted being thoughtful? Reflective?

"It wasn't because I'm talented. Or smart. Like you."

"You see where that got me. I clawed my way to the middle."

"I didn't study the company or the job. I studied the people around me. Picked out the ones who were on the fast track. Became their friend. Did them favors. Made them smile. Fed their egos. And their appetites, sometimes. Kept their secrets. Cleaned up after them."

"And came up with marketing plans that made lots of money."

"I didn't write those plans. I barely passed Marketing 101. But I had swarms of ambitious little MBAs doing the work for me. Trying to impress *me*. I was going where they were hungry to be. A corner office. Stock options. Perks. Delegating failure. Taking credit for success. *O, Paradiso!*"

"What's the matter, Ted?"

He didn't look at me. He kept watching his Martini, as if he expected it to jump off the table and head for the door.

I waited, repeated my question.

"Barry."

That's all he said. Barry is his son. A very successful orthopedic surgeon.

"Is he all right? Is he . . .?"

"He's fine. His family's fine. Nobody's sick or anything. His practice is doing very well."

He finally looked up at me.

"Barry's best friend was in Iraq. He was a nice kid. Not too imaginative, but a nice kid. He went to West Point and became a career officer in the Infantry. He was on patrol in Iraq when an IED almost killed him. They shipped him back. Tried to save him but couldn't. Barry was with him when he died."

He was drinking his Martini too quickly.

"Barry is very good at what he does. He thinks he could have saved his friend if he had been there. In Iraq, I mean. Maybe. Maybe not. But now he's talking about joining the army, so he can be there for other soldiers. On the front lines. Jesus Christ."

"You should be proud of him for feeling that way."

"Who knows what the hell could happen to him over there? Elaine is driving me crazy. Julie, Barry's wife, is frantic. His practice is doing so well." He shook his head. "He can treat these soldiers when they come back to the States. I'm sure he could arrange to do that. But over in a war zone? They don't care if you're a doctor. If you're wearing a uniform, they'll kill you. If you're an American, uniform or not, they'll kill you."

He finished his second Martini, gestured for a third.

I nursed my Manhattan. He might need me to steer him back to the office. Or get him home.

"You can't make his decisions for him."

"If anything happened to him. Losing a child . . ."

"I know."

For the first time that afternoon, he really looked at me.

"I'm sorry, Dave. But you understand."

"Yeah. I understand how Barry feels, too."

He waited for me to explain.

"When I graduated from UConn, I was Phi Beta Kappa, Summa cum laude. I won the English Department prize. I was really hot shit. And I was only twenty years old."

He kept waiting.

"Harvard Graduate School offered me a fellowship. I turned it down. My father never forgave me. For him, that was spitting in God's face."

"Why did you turn it down?"

"A lot of reasons. I was tired of being the good boy. But it wasn't an instant transformation. I also got a fellowship to the University of California in Berkeley."

"I didn't know you went there."

"I went *out* there in August. Stayed at a cheap motel. Saw some great old movies at a grubby little theatre. *The Big Sleep. Grand Hotel. Ninotchka.*"

"You remember the movies you saw?"

"Amazing, isn't it? Nowadays, I'm lucky if I remember what day it is." He almost smiled.

"When I wasn't at the movies, I wandered around Berkeley. That made things worse. All the other students were tan, handsome, beautiful. I wasn't."

I paused for dramatic effect.

"One day, I was at the Post Office, checking out listings for apartment rentals on the bulletin board. Registration was just days away. I made note of a couple of possibilities. As I was leaving, I was greeted by a friendly face. A warm smile."

"A beautiful co-ed?"

"An Army recruiting sergeant."

"In the Post Office?"

"He was in a summer uniform. Bermuda shorts. Neatly-trimmed moustache. Casual, relaxed, honest as the day is long."

"And a good judge of character."

"He was on the prowl. He took one look at me and thought, This kid isn't a happy camper."

"He made the sale."

"He told me about the Army Language School in Monterey, just a short drive from San Francisco. If I passed the language test—which he was sure I would pass—and I got a Top Secret clearance—which he was sure I would get—I could study Russian for a year. Then go to Germany with the Army Security Agency and spend the next two years eavesdropping on the Red Army in East Germany. The Berlin Wall had just been built, so it sounded exciting. Important. And in those days, you owed the Army two years anyway."

"Yeah. I got drafted before things boiled over in Viet Nam. I didn't miss it by much."

"The Army was a good thing for me. I grew up. Traveled. Got to know myself better. Like myself more."

I leaned forward, spoke softly.

"All I'm saying is, there were good reasons for me to join the Army. My father didn't think so. But he never tried to see things from my point of view. And that only made me angrier. More likely to do what he didn't want me to do. Barry has good reasons, too. Don't fight with him about it. Tell him he's right. Tell him you understand how he feels. He should help. He can help. Without leaving his family."

Ted nodded.

"Tell him to volunteer his time—maybe a couple of days a week—at one of the big Army hospitals. Even Walter Reed is only a forty- or fifty-minute shuttle flight away."

I sat back, sipped my Manhattan.

Ted smiled. "You're not as dumb as you look."

"That's what the recruiting sergeant said."

9

Gloria Visits Morty's Castle

The final stop on Gloria Monday's book tour was The Sailor's Castle.

She drew as big a crowd as Buddy D'Amico. The difference: they were all women, mostly middle-aged. One of them had brought her husband. He stared straight ahead, his hands folded in his lap. He wasn't looking for trouble.

The reading/signing was at 1 pm. Gloria was brisk, confident, looked the audience in the eye. She used a portable mike, walking from side to side, making contact, sharing ideas, stimulating questions.

She read a section from her book, underlining words with gestures, expressions. A bravura performance. And it communicated a few simple ideas: men stink, women smell like roses; you don't need men, they need you; don't take any crap, dish it out.

Morty and I and that unfortunate husband were the only males in the crowd. It was like being a Jew at a Nazi rally. Throughout Gloria's remarks, the husband's wife kept looking at him as if he had just raped her. Morty and I stayed out of the line of fire.

When the revels ended, Morty sold a lot of books and Gloria signed her name forty or fifty times. We sat in the now empty book store and shared a pot of fresh-brewed coffee.

"You've really got the touch," I said. "They love you."

She grimaced. "It's just a game. Nothing's spontaneous. I rehearse every move."

"You seem to enjoy it."

She shook her head. "Do you remember that scene in *Lawrence of Arabia*, when Peter O'Toole sticks his hand in the candle flame? And he doesn't pull it out. It's not that it doesn't hurt him. He says, 'The trick is not to let it bother you.' That's the way I do this stuff. On automatic. I don't enjoy it. But I don't let it bother me."

I sighed. "Yeah, it must be a pain in the ass to be admired, idolized. And sell a shitload of books. I wonder if I could endure that."

"You're a bitter old man," Morty said.

"Who's old?"

Gloria laughed.

"Barbara and the baby are coming to visit," Morty said, without much enthusiasm. "That's my daughter," he explained to Gloria. "Her husband's a novelist. Detective fiction. He's written a couple of pretty successful series."

"Clever stuff," I said. "Nice style. One of his detectives is a fencing instructor. Hangs out with a lot of very rich people who murder each other in Rio or St. Moritz or Majorca. They're always drinking wines I've never heard of. At resorts I can't afford. In places I've never been."

"Barbara is a designer. She's very versatile. She's done interior designs for offices, hospitals, hotels. Patterns for textiles, too. She even did some book designs a couple of years ago."

"Are you a frustrated artist?" Gloria asked.

"Frustrated, yes. Artist, no. She got that talent from my wife. Who passed away years ago."

"I think it's great they're coming here," I said.

"Yes, you're right. It *is* great," he agreed, as if he had just made up his mind about it. "She's quite a woman. And I'll get to know my granddaughter."

Gloria sipped her coffee. "I've been meaning to ask you. Why is this 'The Sailor's Castle'? Is that some literary reference I should know? Because I don't."

I groaned.

"Don't worry, David," Morty said. "I won't tell her the whole story."

"Promise?"

Morty focused on Gloria. And of course, he did tell her the whole story.

"When I was a kid, my mother and father were pulling me in opposite directions. My mother was artsycraftsy. She painted watercolors and oils. Wrote poetry. Auditioned for parts in amateur productions. She was truly remarkable: she had absolutely no talent. But she loved beauty. And she tried. God, how she tried."

"And your father was all business?"

"He owned a big retail furniture store. Made good money. Eventually bought a couple more stores. Did very well. And he had a plan. He wanted me to join the business when I graduated from college. Take over for him. So he could retire to Florida."

"And you were stuck in the middle?"

"Yes, but not for long. I went into the business. He retired to Florida. A few years ago, my son took over for me. I retired. And that brings us to The Sailor's Castle."

"Finally," I said.

"When I was a kid, my mother used to tell me a story. I'm pretty sure she made it up herself. About a poor family that lived in a big city by the sea. This was back in the days of the sailing ships. The father was a shoemaker, who barely made a living. His wife helped out, working as a seamstress. They had two sons. The older boy picked up odd jobs whenever he could. The younger boy preferred to steal things."

"Boys will be boys," I said.

"On the older boy's twelfth birthday, he decided to ease the burden on his parents. So he ran away to sea on a ship that was sailing to China.

"For the next twenty years, he traveled around the world. It was an endless adventure. Meeting all kinds of people. Seeing things he had never even dreamed of. The Great Wall of China. The Taj Mahal. The Pyramids. Icebergs, jungles, deserts.

"And after twenty years, he finally came home. He knew that his parents had died long ago. And he had lost track of his younger brother. But when he came ashore he quickly discovered that his brother—by hook, but mostly by crook—had become the wealthiest, most powerful man in the city, one who was hated and feared. And he lived in a huge castle on a rocky hill above the city.

"The castle was guarded by a troop of soldiers who stopped the sailor at the gate. When he told them who he was, they got word to his brother and the sailor was allowed to enter the castle. He was led into an enormous, high-ceilinged room, filled with richly-dressed men and women. His brother, more richly dressed than any of them, was sitting on a chair that looked a lot like a throne. He had a nasty expression on his face. And instead of welcoming his older brother, he began to brag. He said, 'Look around you. I'm at the top of the heap. Wealth. Power. I've got it all. And I live in this beautiful castle. What do you have?'

"The sailor smiled and said, 'I live in a bigger and more beautiful castle than you've ever seen. The sailor's castle is the sea.'"

"The sailor's castle," Gloria said.

"My mother kept telling me to build my castle, whatever it was. And not worry about money."

"You went into your father's business anyway," she said.

"But I always dreamed of owning a bookstore. Like this one. That's my mother's side of me. It wasn't practical. Still isn't. But when I retired, I said, It's time to build my castle. So I did."

"I may cry," I said.

"You *are* a bitter old man," Gloria said, half seriously.

"And proud of it."

"What about your castle, David?" Gloria asked. "Did you ever build it?"

"That's what I've been doing for the past four or five years. My books."

Her eyes narrowed. "Speaking of your books, how's it going? Your new novel."

"I'm making progress."

"Progress, huh?"

"He's been very excited about it," Morty (*Loose lips sink ships*) said. "Working long hours. I didn't see him for a couple of weeks."

I dismissed the remark with a contemptuous wave of the hand. "What the hell does he know?"

Gloria swooped down like a hungry eagle. "I want to see it."

"I didn't say it was ready to be seen. It may never be ready."

"Who the hell do you think you are: Emily Dickinson? Take a chance. Let me read it."

"Gloria, cease and desist."

She frowned. "Okay, Emily. But if I can't see your castle, I want to see your house."

"My house?"

"I invited you to my place, remember? I want you to invite me to your place. Now. Yeah, why not now? For a drink. Maybe two. I think I'm entitled to that."

"She's right," Morty said.

"Did I ask for your opinion?"

"Invite me," she said.

"Maybe I'll run away to sea."

She laughed. "You're too old to be a cabin boy."

"So I'll be a cabin man."

"Take me to your house."

I bobbed and weaved. "Do you know what the Martian said to Franz Schubert? 'Take me to your Lieder.'"

Gloria began to sing, *"C'mona my house, my house, I'm gonna give you candy . . ."*

I raised my hands in surrender.

"Okay, Gloria. C'mona my house."

10

Gloria Visits My Garden

I unlocked my front door and reached inside to click on the hall light. "*Après vous.*"

Edging around her, I went into the living room, switched on the standing lamp and beckoned for her to enter.

As she scanned the premises, I increased the wattage, switching on a table lamp.

"Who was your decorator? Duffy of San Quentin?"

"I suppose it's kind of low key."

"Kind of? How long have you lived here?"

"About five-six years."

"Have you ever considered warming the place up a little? Like maybe a couple of throw pillows. A plant. Or hanging a painting or two on the wall?"

"There's a painting in the bedroom."

"No sense overdoing it."

"Would you like a glass of wine?"

"In a festive environment like this, how can I refuse?"

"Pinot Noir? Chardonnay?"

"Anything alcoholic. Please."

She sat on the couch. I poured a glass of Pinot Noir for each of us.

"This would be an ideal spot for self-flagellation. Do Jews do that?"

"Only figuratively."

I gave her a glass of wine and sat down opposite her.

She drank a little, looked around some more, drank some more.

"I know you've been dreaming of Provence, but might I suggest Devil's Island? If that's still a going business."

"Who the hell do I have to impress? All I care about is comfort."

"I get the message. But you may be overplaying it." Pause. "You didn't live this way when you were married."

"I let my wives pick the furniture, the drapes, the rest of the crap. My only requirement was an extra firm mattress."

"Do you really mean that? I can't decide whether to be *im*pressed or *de*pressed."

Gloria sipped her wine, watched me for a moment, said, "New subject. I have a question. I've been in love a few times. I've had some long-term relationships. Lived with people. But I've never been married. That's different, I guess. Isn't it? How does it feel to be married?"

"Depends on the marriage."

"What about your marriages?"

"The first time, I was acting in somebody else's play. Pretending. I never felt at home. My first wife, Karen, came from money. Her father subsidized us. Actually bought us an apartment on the East Side. Expensive furniture. Fancy schmancy. I was living in a museum. I tiptoed around, afraid I would spill something, or break something. After a few months, I carved out a sanctuary for myself. A den that was more my style . . ."

"Barren, grim, somber."

"Let's just call it 'informal.' I could relax there."

"You poor bastard."

"The furniture was a symptom. I didn't feel at home with Karen either. Never got close to her. I kept trying to break through the walls she had built around herself. It turned out that the walls *were* her. I had invented the person I married. And it wasn't Karen."

"Ah, romance."

"I wasn't fair to her. I wore her out."

"Okay, exit Wife Number One. Nightmare's over. Enter Wife Number Two."

I thought for a moment, drained my wine glass, refilled it and hers. "Mandy and I had been close friends since we were kids. We grew up on the same block. In college and after college, we kept in touch. Told each other everything. I couldn't confide in anyone else. Not my other friends. My sister. Or, Godhelpme, my parents. Only Mandy. But I never dated her."

"Why not?"

"I don't know. We were the same age. In high school and college—in those days, anyway—girls usually went out with older guys."

"But you finally caught up with each other."

"By then, she was divorced. I was getting a divorce. And I had a brainstorm: all my life, I had been comparing the women I met to Mandy. If she was the standard, why settle for less?"

"Makes sense."

"I guess I had loved her all my life. She wasn't so sure about me. It took me almost a year to convince her."

"Sounds like a happy ending. What went wrong?"

"I'll tell you someday. Not today, Gloria. If you don't mind."

"A brief summary will do. A hint."

"I'd rather not."

"Secret manuscripts. Secret lives. You should have been in the C.I.A."

She pointed to the far corner of the room.

"Do I see a guitar case leaning against the wall? Or is that a secret, too?"

"It's a guitar case."

"I assume there's a guitar in it. It can't be a decoration. Nothing in this house is."

"I play a little."

"If this were a movie, you would pick up that guitar and perform a Bach partita the way Andres Segovia only dreamed of playing it."

"This isn't a movie. I play badly. I can accompany folk songs. Simple folk songs. For simple folk."

"Are you just being modest?"

"Believe me, I have a lot to be modest about. I stole that line from Churchill."

"I promise not to tell him. You sing, too, I presume."

"About as well as I play."

"You won't let me read your novel. Would you at least sing me a song?"

"After I have a little more wine. For courage. Meanwhile, I'll tell you how I learned to be a troubadour."

I replenished our wine glasses.

"When I graduated from college, I joined the army. You said I should have been in the C.I.A. You're a good judge of talent. I did the Cloak-and-Dagger thing. In the army equivalent of the N.S.A. The Army Security Agency."

"Never heard of it."

"This was back in the early Sixties. Sixty-one. Sixty-two. Before you were born. The Cold War was getting hotter. We were eavesdropping on the Russian army in East Germany. We didn't have spy satellites and all that sophisticated stuff. The technology was really primitive. We sent planes over East Germany to intercept Russian radio messages. One of the planes was shot down while I was there. A buddy of mine was killed."

"So that was what you did? Fly over East Germany?"

"No. I was back at the base. Translating what was recorded. Trying to figure out what the Russians were up to."

"Where did you learn Russian? In college?"

"At the Army Language School in Monterey. Before Silicon Valley, Monterey was still a small town. A fishing village. There was a working cannery down on Cannery Row. You could smell it. John Steinbeck would have felt right at home."

"It's a tourist trap now."

"I know. I went back a few years ago."

"You learned Russian there."

"Seven different instructors a day for about a year. They were Russians. From different regions. Different accents. You learned how to speak the language the way a child does. Memorizing phrases. Saying things before you can read. Before you know any grammar. Then gradually learning the rules. It works."

"Did they also teach you how to play the guitar?"

"No. I picked that up my last year in college. At the Language school, I met a guy who played the five-string banjo. And another who played the guitar about as well as I did, which wasn't all that great. But we started to sing together. In the barracks. On the beach. Even did a couple of songs at a coffee house down on Cannery Row where they had an amateur night. We sounded pretty good. I could sing tenor harmony. And the other guitar player chimed in once in a while with some nice baritone harmony."

"A trio is born."

"Folk music was just beginning to go mainstream. The Kingston Trio.

Peter, Paul and Mary. Meanwhile, in San Francisco, the beat generation was turning into hippies. Drugs. Sex. And protest songs, too, although before Viet Nam, the protests were generic. Anti-Establishment. Anti-Business."

The wine in my glass had disappeared. I was beginning to mellow out. I poured another.

"We sang a lot of *old* protest songs. Pete Seeger. Woody Guthrie. 'We Shall Not Be Moved.' 'Down By the Riverside.' 'Union Maid.' That's m-a-i-d."

I sang (unaccompanied):

"There once was a Union maid,
"Who never was afraid
"Of goons and ginks
"And company finks
"And deputy sheriffs who made the raid.

"She went to the Union hall
"When a meeting it was called.
"And when the Legion boys came 'round
"You'd always hear her say,

"Oh, you can't scare me
"I'm stickin' to the Union, etc., etc."

"You have a nice voice."

"I think those were the words. I don't remember them all. We even played one professional gig. I'll tell you about it someday."

"Will wonders never cease." She pointed at the guitar case. "Are you ready to play that partita?"

I fortified myself with another mouthful of wine, put down the glass and got up to fetch the case. I watched her smile as I tuned the strings.

"Tell you what I'll do. I'll play you one song. A song I wrote way back when."

"You're a composer, too?"

"I was. For a little while. I like this one."

I sang (accompanied):

"The sun smiles on my garden day or night.
"My garden's always bright
"And warm as spring.
"The flowers never die, no autumn there,
"Their perfume fills the air.
"It makes me sing.

"My garden's where I go to dream,
"To rest beside a crystal stream.
"To paint a picture, write a poem.
"My garden's where my heart's at home,
"My heart's at home.

"The wings of butterflies and honey bees
"Create a gentle breeze
"That stirs the leaves.
"No one can hurt me here,
"I'm safe and sound.
"I feel love all around,
"The spell it weaves.

"My garden's where I go to dream,
"To rest beside a crystal stream.
"To drink the sweet, cool morning dew.
"I love my garden,
"And my garden is you."

After I finished, Gloria watched me for a minute or two. She looked down at my hands cradling the guitar, resting lightly on the strings.

"That's very romantic." She smiled. "From a cynic like you?"

"I told you I wrote it a long time ago."

"For someone, of course."

"Yes."

"Wife Number Two?"

I shrugged, neither confirming nor denying.

She could think that I wrote it for Mandy. She didn't have to know the truth. Not yet.

Maybe never.

May 12, 1962
Fresh Air Camp Trio Dies in San Jose

The Monterey Peninsula. A triangular chunk of California jutting into the Pacific Ocean, cradling Monterey Bay in its arms.

Nineteen sixty-two, long before the high-tech explosion of Silicon Valley. The peninsula is both high-roller territory and John Steinbeck country.

For high rollers: on the western tip of the triangle, the Pebble Beach golf course. To the south, Carmel-by-the-Sea, wealthy, ultraprivate, strictly policed. A Frank-Lloyd-Wright house on the beach where *A Summer Place* was filmed.

But in the northern elbow of the peninsula, in the town of Monterey, John Steinbeck could still feel at home. A quiet fishing village on the Bay. The old Custom House on Alvorado Street, a relic of California's Spanish roots. A handful of modest seafood restaurants by the shore. Fishing boats sailing out every morning. The potent aroma of a working cannery down on Cannery Row.

There was fog almost every morning and evening. And hot sun almost every afternoon. It was rainy in the winter. Dry the rest of the year.

A few miles to the northeast on the mainland was Fort Ord, mainly sand dunes. An infantry training center for 25,000 troops.

About one hundred miles to the north was San Francisco (not to mention Berkeley). It was the hey-day of The North Beach and Haight-Ashbury. A parallel universe of Hippies (nee The Beat Generation): Ginsberg, Cassady, Ferlinghetti and all their disciples, imitators, camp-followers. A time of free verse and free love—straight/gay/bi/tri. Of pot and Lucy in the Sky with Diamonds. And all the pre-Vietnam-War seeds of the protest movement were already sprouting.

Back in Monterey, at the Presidio on the hill overlooking the town was the Army Language School. Housed in wooden, two-story, green-roofed World-War-II barracks, still going strong. There were hundreds of soldiers, a scattering of sailors and marines. They were mostly enlisted men, PFCs, short-timers. Plus some non-commissioned officers, lieutenants, captains: a year in California was their reward for services rendered.

It was an uneasy, uncomfortable time. The temperature of the Cold War was spiking. The Berlin Wall had been built less than a year ago. The Bay of Pigs invasion was a disaster. And worse: the USSR's test of a hydrogen bomb was the biggest, baddest man-made explosion in history. (The Cuban Missile Crisis was just around the corner.)

Hundreds of soldiers at the Army Language School were learning Russian. Private First Class Daniel Berman was one of them.

He had graduated from NYU with honors: *summa cum laude, Phi Beta Kappa*, English Department prize. He didn't attend the graduation ceremony. (Dad: "You're crazy!") He applied for and won a Harvard GSAS scholarship and turned it down. In his father's eyes, this was a crime on a par with genocide, or maybe even Original Sin.

He applied for and won a scholarship to the University of California, Berkeley. He went to Berkeley. Never registered.

Stop the merry-go-round! I want to get off. Why not reach for the gold ring? Do I really need a gold ring?

That's when he joined the army.

He called Amy first. She understood. He called Carol second. She said she understood. He called Dad third. He didn't understand.

Daniel took basic training at Fort Ord, an Easterner among Westerners. It was a cliché movie platoon: a slow-talking cowboy from Montana, a stoic Indian from Arizona, a lanky carpenter from Texas, a nature freak from Oregon, a streetsmart black kid from Oakland. Drop-outs, drifters, returning veterans who couldn't make a go of it in the real world.

Most were draftees. The serial numbers on their dog tags started with *US.* Daniel had enlisted. His serial number started with *RA* (Regular Army). He had a three-year hitch ahead of him. The draftees, only two years. They mocked him: "RA all the way!"

Daniel wasn't in great physical shape. He had never been much of a jock. But he sure as hell got into great shape. At the end of ten weeks, he could run for two miles without breathing hard. Became a Marksman (*but not a Sharpshooter, damn it!*) with an M1 gas-operated semi-automatic clip-fed .30 caliber Garand rifle. Could disassemble and assemble the M1 rifle in less than a minute. (So could everyone else.)

Got a tan and a crewcut.

After eight weeks confined to the base, Daniel and five of his buddies in Army Green dress uniforms went out to eat at a posh Carmel restaurant. Each of them ordered a full-course steak dinner. (The first real food they'd had in two months.) Finished it. Smoked a cheap cigar. Ordered a second steak dinner. Finished it. Smoked a second cheap cigar. Left the maitre d' and waiters in a state of shock.

While he was in Basic, he took the Army Language School test. He had a talent for languages. He had studied Spanish, German, Latin.

He called Amy that night. "Very clever test. They created an artificial language. To start with, they give you a simple vocabulary. A little grammar. For every question, they add more words. More grammatical rules. By the time you reach the last question, it's almost like translating Virgil from Latin."

"Sounds very hard. For mere mortals like me."

"I think I aced it."

"You smug bastard."

He aced it.

And he got a Top Secret clearance, too. ("No surprise. I've led a very dull life.")

Next stop: a few miles down the coast. Monterey. The Russian language. After that, what would he actually be doing? He could guess, but he didn't yet have a need to know. They'd tell him when the time came.

■■■

Daniel woke up early on that Saturday morning, May 12, 1962. He could have slept late. On weekends at the Army Language School, your time was your own (unless you were on the K.P. roster).

Daniel hadn't slept well.

Tonight is the night. God help us.

He looked down the row of bunks. Leo Morse was still sleeping, but Mike Dixon was already gone. He was probably at Dee's, the diner just outside the Presidio. (The food in the mess hall was terrible.)

Forty minutes later, showered, shaved, in jeans and a sweatshirt, Daniel walked into Dee's and found Mike eating breakfast at the counter.

Mike was stocky, square-jawed, intense. He was usually withdrawn. You might even say *aloof*. If he needed you, he was friendly. He needed

Daniel and Leo. Sure, Mike played a mean five-string banjo. But all by himself, he couldn't be a trio.

"*Dobraya ootra* (Good morning)," Daniel said.

(<u>Note</u>: It was customary for Army Language School students to speak Russian to each other much of the time, on or off duty. Good practice for them. Not for us. From now on, to keep things moving, we'll stick to English.)

"Is Leo up yet?"

"Still sleeping. I guess he's not worried."

"Are you?"

"Yeah."

"We'll do fine."

Daniel ordered scrambled eggs, sausages, home fries, toast and coffee.

"I spoke to Eleanor last night," Mike said.

Eleanor was Mike's fiancée, a senior at San Jose State.

"You're still talking to her?"

"We'll drive to San Jose this morning. Pick up the girls at the sorority house. Have lunch with them."

"Then can we strangle them?"

"We'll go over to the club this afternoon. Check it out."

"Keep the motor running in your car tonight. So we can make a fast getaway."

"We'll do fine."

Daniel grunted. Mike smiled.

Daniel's breakfast arrived.

"I forgot to tell you," Mike said. "A couple of days ago, the guy who runs the place asked Eleanor for the name of the trio, so he could make up a sign."

"I can see the headline in *The Monterey Herald*: 'FRESH AIR CAMP TRIO DIES IN SAN JOSE'."

Daniel, Mike and Leo lived on the second floor of the barracks where the windows were always open. The windows on the first floor were always closed. Most of the soldiers on the first floor were from California. They were indolent. Sunbathed constantly. And they slept with the windows shut. So they called the upper floor of the barracks "The Fresh Air Camp."

"She didn't remember what we call ourselves," Mike said. "She made up a name: The Boys and I."

"The Boys and I? Which one of us isn't a boy?"

Mike laughed. "Well, Leo still hasn't made up his mind."

Leo's interest in women was marginal, at best. And he didn't seem to be interested in men, either.

"But why the hell didn't she ask you first?" Daniel took a savage bite of toast. "Jesus! She shouldn't have booked us into that place. We're not professional musicians. What the hell was she thinking? We're going to look like idiots."

Mike shrugged.

Daniel shoveled eggs and sausages into his mouth. Washed the food down with coffee. Snorted.

"The whole thing is disgusting. Humiliating. And don't say, 'We'll do fine.'"

"We will."

Mike flipped the pages of the juke box selector on the counter. At Dee's, all the music was Country and Western. Mike dropped a quarter in the slot, played three songs.

When Patsy Cline began her swooping, nasal "I Fall to Pieces," Daniel said, "My sentiments exactly."

"Danny, we've done these songs a hundred times. We sounded pretty good last night, didn't we?"

They had rehearsed in one of the classrooms.

"Pretty good? It's not like playing for our friends in the barracks. Or on the beach. We're getting paid."

"Hey, this isn't Carnegie Hall. It's a pizza joint. A bunch of kids from the college. They'll be drinking, ready to have a good time. We're just glorified background noise."

"They could turn into an ugly mob."

"Is there any point in rehearsing this morning?"

"We should save our voices," Daniel said.

"I figure we'll leave for San Jose around ten-thirty."

"Let's go wake Leo up. How the hell can he sleep at a time like this?"

"I'll ask him."

When they woke him up, Leo didn't seem to remember that the Fresh Air Camp Trio was playing its first professional gig that night at a hangout for students at San Jose State.

"Is it Saturday already?" he yawned.

Leo Morse was slow-moving, soft-spoken.

He was a puzzle that Daniel didn't want to solve. Leo spoke about himself often, but impersonally, as if he were talking about someone else.

He said that he was born in England to American parents. Raised in France. His father and mother owned an art gallery on the *Rive Gauche* in Paris (he said). He had never attended college. "My folks taught me everything I know."

That's what he said. But maybe none of it was true.

Mike Dixon and Leo Morse. Not Daniel's best buddies. No way. Show business makes strange bedfellows.

●●●

Mike's car was a ten-year-old Chevy station wagon with God knows how many miles on it. (In fact, only God knew. The odometer was stuck at 96,000.) Mike had inherited it from his older brother. The engine didn't purr. It snarled. It burned gas at an astonishing rate. The chassis was bent, dented and rusted. The tires had seen much better days. With a little luck, the car would survive the seventy miles to San Jose and back. Daniel hoped that he would, too.

Two guitars and a five-string banjo were stowed in the cargo area. Mike and Leo sat in front. Daniel opted for the back seat: the condemned man preferred to be alone with his thoughts.

His thoughts. So much had happened in the past year. So many changes. So many decisions, crowded into a few months. He was becoming someone else. Stronger. More comfortable with himself. With women, too.

There was a club on Cannery Row, *The Outrigger*. A bar and restaurant downstairs. A dance floor upstairs. He was there most Friday and Saturday nights. Tentative at first, and then aided and abetted by two or three beers, he began to relax. To meet women. To leave with them.

He got to first or second base. Sometimes even third. But he rarely hit a home run, for two reasons. First, hippiedom notwithstanding, for most young women this was still old-fashioned morality time. And it was pre-Pill. Single girls didn't trust men to be careful. And for single girls, pregnancy was the ultimate deal-killer. Second, Daniel wasn't very aggressive. He was romantic. He didn't have to love a girl, but she had to be someone he might possibly fall in love with. It wasn't macho, but it was him.

A couple of times, with a few sadder-but-wiser women, he satisfied himself. Afterwards, he had a story to tell. But he always felt an aftertaste of emptiness. Disgust. He knew why those women were sadder but wiser.

He tried not to think about tonight's show. He was sorry that Linda Grant would be there. But he wasn't sorry that he would see her again.

Linda was Eleanor's sorority sister. A virgin who successfully defended her virginity. She was pretty. Almost as tall as Daniel. Slim and strong. Soft. He could close his eyes and feel that soft strength in his fingertips. And feel tenderness toward her.

Eleanor had introduced them a couple of months ago. He had seen her four or five times since then. When they touched, kissed, held each other close, she was as feverish as he was. When she said, "No more," she always shook her head, as if she were contradicting what she said.

Tonight, she would be there to watch the Fresh Air Camp Trio die in San Jose.

···

They picked up the girls at the Kappa Delta house and went to a burger place for lunch.

The vibes weren't great. Mike and Eleanor were not quite as lovey-dovey as usual. Leo and his date—a bouncy, pudgy, very non-Leo type named Kathy Kearns—tolerated each other.

But Daniel couldn't be angry at Linda. He sat close to her, touched her shoulder or her hair now and then, smiled at her.

She said, softly, "You're not really mad at me, are you?"

"It's not your fault."

"What if it was my fault?"

"I wouldn't be mad at you anyway."

She took his hand.

He said, "I hope we don't screw up tonight."

"You won't. I've heard you. You're very good."

Mike was watching them. He nodded approvingly.

"The deal is, we're getting ten bucks a piece," he said. "Plus all the pizza and beer we want."

"Not a bad deal," Eleanor said.

"All the pizza I can eat?" Kathy said. "All the beer I can drink? I'm ready, Freddy!"

"Eat fast," Daniel said. "We may be kicked out after the first show."

"We'll do fine," Mike said.

After they brought the girls back to Kappa Delta, they drove to *Antonio's*, a pizza parlor/club downtown. It was a one-story, whitewashed brick building with a colorful painting of an Italian landscape decorating the front wall. There was a large parking lot in the back. A hand-lettered cardboard sign was posted at the entrance:

Saturday, May 12
Tonight Only!
Sing along with
THE BOYS AND I!
Folk Singing Trio
First Show: 8:30 pm

"Good Lord," Daniel said.

"Be cool now," Mike warned.

Carrying their instruments, they entered a long, high-ceilinged room filled with a couple dozen tables. At the center of the room was a bandstand with three chairs, three music stands, three microphones on it. At the back of the room, near the doors to the kitchen, was a bar. Two men were seated there, drinking beer.

The bartender saw them, came out and met them.

"You the guys playing here tonight?" he said.

Mike nodded.

"Antonio Rossi," he said, shaking Mike's hand, then Leo's, then Daniel's. "The dressing room is over there." He pointed to a door a few feet from the bar. "You want to check out the sound system? I set it up already. Give it a try. I can adjust it."

"Yeah. Thanks," Mike said.

They went to the bandstand, took out their instruments, sat down, pretended to tune them.

Mike said, "*This Land Is Your Land.*"

It was the first song they had sung together months ago. They could play it in their sleep.

Zero hour, Daniel thought.

Mike plucked the opening solo phrase. Daniel's and Leo's guitars picked up the beat. They began singing.

Daniel couldn't believe what he heard.

The microphones made everything easier. Better. They didn't have to strain their voices. The sound of the banjo was sharper and tighter. The sound of the guitars was smoother and richer.

The two men came over from the bar and sat at a table by the bandstand. Mike said to Antonio, "Sounds fine." To Daniel and Leo, "*Tijuana Jail.*"

Smooth. Funny.

"*We Shall Not Be Moved.*"

Proud. Soaring.

The music filled the empty room.

Antonio Rossi was tapping his feet. The two men at the table were doing the same.

At the end of the song, one of the men at the table said, "We'll be back."

Mike said, "We'll see you tonight."

Daniel felt a little better. But only a little.

■■■

That night. 8:25 pm. *Antonio's* was packed with noisy college students. Eleanor, Linda and Kathy were at a table next to the bandstand.

Daniel, Mike and Leo were in the dressing room, a windowless walk-in closet furnished with a chair, a bench and a table. A mirror hung on the wall behind the table.

They had changed into their Fresh Air Camp Trio outfits: khaki chinos, white long-sleeved shirts, a green garter on the left sleeve.

"We'll start with *This Land,*" Mike said. "I've got the list. I'll put it on the music stand. I'll probably follow it. But I may switch things around."

"Okay," Daniel said.

He looked at his image in the mirror. A pale, gaunt stranger.

"Ready?" Mike asked.

Daniel and Leo nodded.

They heard Antonio's introduction.

"Ladies and gentlemen! Tonight, for one night only, *Antonio's* is proud to present a great new folksinging trio! Let's hear it for The Boys and I!"

Mike opened the door of the dressing room and walked out. Leo followed him. It took only a moment for Daniel to join them.

In that moment, it seemed as if there were thousands of young people in the restaurant, moving in slow motion. All of them staring at him. Their applause sounded distant and hollow. The bandstand was like a nightmare goal: it kept moving further away from him. His legs were shaky, his knees knocking. He was gasping for air.

He climbed onto the bandstand as if it were a life raft. He sat down, rested his guitar on his thigh, gripped the neck tightly, stared at Mike's list of songs on the music stand and waited to die.

After what seemed like a thousand years, Mike said, "*This Land Is Your Land*," and began to play.

Daniel and Leo joined him.

Something strange happened. He was playing and singing, but he was in the audience, too. He heard their music. The nervous, rippling rhythm of the banjo. The solid beat of the guitars. His tenor harmony, riding over the melody, sweetening the sound.

The noisy students quieted down. Daniel looked at the faces around him. They were watching, listening, enjoying, singing the chorus. He found Linda's face. She smiled at him.

We'll do fine, he thought. *We'll do fine*.

By the time they had finished the song, as the audience applauded, Daniel felt completely at ease. Three minutes of music and all the fear had drained away. He was a musician. An entertainer.

Mike turned to him and said, "Let's build a little momentum. Let's do *Union Maid*. It's funny. They'll love it. We'll do a slow number after that."

He nodded.

They loved it.

The first show—there were three scheduled—twenty songs, about an hour, was over too quickly.

Mike told the audience, "We're taking a break. Be back in twenty minutes."

They sat at the table with the girls.

Linda kissed Daniel on the cheek. He put his arm around her, kissed her mouth lightly.

"You were great," she said.

Kathy said, "You guys rock!"

She tried to kiss Leo, who managed to move out of range.

Mike and Eleanor shared two or three very hot kisses, then attacked the pizza together.

Daniel drained a bottle of beer, put down his half-eaten slice of pizza and took Linda's hand. "Come outside with me."

He led her around the front of Antonio's into the shadows on the side of the building. He leaned against the wall and pulled her into his arms. Held her close. Kissed her. Tasted traces of tomato sauce and beer in her breath.

He looked up at a jagged smear of stars above them. He wished that he knew the name of every one of those stars. A fresh, gentle California breeze caressed his face, reminding him that he was still very young, with most of his life ahead of him. This was only the beginning.

So many possibilities, he thought. *Things I can't even imagine yet. People I'll meet. Women I'll make love to. So much time. So much future.*

"*Maya krasivaya dyevushka,*" he whispered in Linda's ear.

"Is that dirty?" she asked.

"No. It means 'my beautiful girl'."

She tightened her arms around him, kissed his mouth.

It doesn't get better than this, he thought.

It didn't.

11

Seagulls Dreaming of Japan

In Fairfield, the third week in June felt like August. Too hot. Sticky. Not my cup of tea. I may write songs about the sun shining on my garden, but that's poetry. Life is prose.

When people get to be my age, most of them head south automatically, like migrating birds. Not me. I don't boat or fish, and I don't play tennis any more: bad rotator cuff. And when it comes to elective surgery to repair it, I vote *No*.

Unfortunately, the sun does bad things to my skin. My youthful sunburns have caught up to me with a vengeance. I'm my dermatologist's delight. I keep sprouting new problems and he keeps slicing them off and sending them to Yale-New Haven Hospital to make sure they're benign. So far, a couple have been problematic. Borderline. Stay tuned for further developments.

"That'll be a $25 co-pay, please. See you in six months."

On sunny summer days, I wear a cap, long-sleeved buttoned-up shirt, shades, sunscreen on any exposed epidermis. The Elephant Man out for a stroll.

So I'll never migrate with the snowbirds. And I won't die in Miami or Phoenix. Which is fine with me: they're both boring cities.

On the other hand, Ms. Gloria Monday loved the beach. Scoffed at skin cancer, as if that were enough to immunize her. Sunbathed and swam at the little strip of sand in Southport. Went to Southampton to spend a beachy week or two with friends.

She and her freckles got tan. Her hair got redder. She called me Pale-Face.

Now and then she asked me about my novel. I maintained a dignified silence. And kept writing.

We went to the movies some afternoons at one of the local multiplexes.

We were often the only people in the theatre. Sometimes, if the movie wasn't to our liking, we sneaked into another theatre (also empty). Our record was four in an afternoon, and we didn't see more than a half hour of any of them.

We also went to three Broadway shows (two on one Wednesday). Gloria got us great seats. She knew people. Choreographers. Directors. Actors. Angels. She was connected.

We went backstage a couple of times. Which was disappointing. The dressing rooms were gloomy. Grim. ("You must feel right at home," Gloria said.) We met the actors. They were rarely as handsome or beautiful up close. Bad skin. And always watching themselves through other peoples' eyes.

Once, long ago, I went backstage at the Metropolitan Opera at Lincoln Center. I was a friend of a friend of one of the baritones. Backstage there was not quite as disappointing. But also austere. Functional.

The real fun in going backstage is walking past the peasants who *can't* get in. Your name is on a list. You're somebody. Or at least, they think you're somebody.

The story of my life.

Late in July, Morty's daughter, Barbara, arrived from California with Niki to spend a couple of weeks with him. Her husband stayed home. He was on deadline to complete his latest novel. My publisher is less pushy with me: I wonder why.

Barbara joined us for morning bagels and coffee. With Niki, too, who was a very pretty, much too calm two-year-old. Serene almost. I found that a little unnerving. Kids her age are usually jumpier, messier, more defiant.

She echoed her mother. Barbara was someone you might not notice at first. Until you looked closely. Slender, small: an inch over five feet tall. Finely boned face, very large, dark eyes. She spoke softly, slowly, but not hesitantly, as if she were considering every word very carefully before she said it.

"Do you miss Connecticut?" I asked her on the morning we met.

She shook her head. "I miss my Dad and my brother. Otherwise, no.

Connecticut's too comfortable with itself. A long time ago, it decided what it was going to be. What it will always be."

She sipped her coffee. Cut her bagel in half.

"California can't make up its mind. It's too big. Too rich. Too poor." (Sip.) "Too beautiful. Too ugly."

She spread cream cheese on each half of the bagel.

"It's always on the edge of disaster. Forest fires. Earthquakes. Droughts. Mud slides."

She carefully bit off a small piece of creamcheesed bagel, chewed it, swallowed it.

"Connecticut looks east. Toward the Atlantic Ocean. An old-fashioned, sentimental ocean."

"Sentimental?" I wondered.

"The Gulf Stream is so warm and fuzzy."

She smiled.

"In California, it's the Pacific. Which is anything but warm and fuzzy."

She nodded, agreeing with herself in advance.

"It's hot. Surrounded by volcanoes. The Rim of Fire. Unpredictable. Dangerous."

She took another bite, chewed, swallowed.

"That's more my style."

"Dangerous?" I said.

She smiled again. "Unpredictable."

Morty was holding Niki on his lap, kissing her head occasionally. He was watching Barbara the way I knew he must have watched her mother.

The way I used to watch Lisa.

Barbara reminded me of Lisa. Not physically. The way she looked at the world. At seagulls dreaming of Japan.

Lisa. In a few weeks, it would be the tenth of August, a date I always marked but never celebrated.

I'm always alone on that day, I thought. *Maybe I shouldn't be.*

"Isn't that what creativity is?" Barbara said. "Being unpredictable. Doing the unexpected. That's what my clients like about my designs."

Niki asked, "Daddy coming soon?"

"No, sweetheart," Barbara said. "Daddy had to stay home. He has work to do. We're going home soon."

Niki clapped her hands and laughed. "Home soon."

"But not too soon," Morty said and kissed Niki.

"Too soon, too soon," Niki said and clapped her hands again.

"Dad tells me you're a writer."

"He's one of the few people in the world who knows it. I'm late to the game, and not exactly a major player."

Barbara put her small hand on my shoulder. "As long as you enjoy doing it. As long as it gives you pleasure."

"It does."

"For Jeff, writing began as an art." She frowned. "But now it's become a craft."

"I've read a couple of his novels," I said. "He's a good storyteller. Very stylish."

"But too safe, unwilling to make the leap."

"He sells a lot of books. Has an army of fans. Nothing wrong with that," Morty said.

"Amen," I said.

"He could do better. Do more. He has the talent. When I met him," she remembered, "he was working on a wonderful story. About twin brothers growing up in Chicago in the 1940's. But it wasn't a real Chicago. It was half real, half magical."

She pointed a finger at herself.

"My fault. We got married. He never finished it. He decided that making money was his top priority."

"Isn't it?" Morty asked.

Barbara didn't answer him. Her dark eyes did.

"He's still young," I said. "One of these days, he may finish that book."

"I'm not sure he could do it now. He's become more Atlantic. Less Pacific. He's predictable. He knows what his audience expects. He doesn't want to disappoint them. It's like painting by the numbers."

"Have you told him how you feel?" Morty asked.

"He says not to worry. He can cut loose any time he wants to."

"So why worry?"

"I don't believe it. I don't think he does, either."

Niki reached out for Barbara. "Mommy, Mommy."

Morty lowered Niki gently to her feet. She ran to her mother, who picked her up, hugged her, resettled her on a new lap.

"Have a little faith," Morty said.

"Little, little," Niki whispered. "Big, BIG!" she shouted.

Barbara hugged her tighter, shouted, "Big, BIG!"

We all shouted, "Big, BIG!"

We all laughed.

At ten that night, I called Mandy. She wasn't at home, or she wasn't answering the phone. I called her office number. She answered.

"Working late, as usual?"

"You know me. I don't need much sleep." Wide awake. Self-assured.

"Yeah, I know."

"I'm rewriting a brief. Editing it, really."

"If I'm calling at a bad time . . ."

"No. I could use a break. What's up, Doc?"

I laughed. "I haven't heard that since I don't know when. It was her favorite gag when she was nine, ten."

"I guess . . ."

"I remember Lisa telling her friends that both of her parents were doctors. She said a JD was a Junior Doctor. And a PhD was a Phony Doctor. And neither of us could cure anything."

"Yes, I remember." She suddenly sounded tired.

"We sure as hell couldn't cure her."

Silence.

"I'm calling about Lisa," I said.

Silence.

"Her birthday is in a couple of weeks. I thought maybe you and I— maybe Philip, too—could get together for dinner. Not a celebration, exactly. Just to think about her. Talk about her. Together."

Silence.

"We've never done that," I said. "Isn't it time to do that?"

"I don't think so."

"Why not?"

"I look at that picture all the time," she said, so softly I could hardly hear her.

She meant the photograph of our family that hung in Philip's living room. That was on her desk at the office. That I carried in my wallet. The only picture I carried.

"So do I," I said.

"There's no reason to have a birthday party."

"I said it wouldn't be a party."

"No, David. It's not a good idea."

"But it's been so long. There are things you or Philip may remember about her that I've forgotten. I don't want to forget anything about her."

"What can we say that we haven't already said? That we love her? That we miss her? That it isn't fair? What the hell is the point of it?"

"I don't want to be alone again. On her birthday."

"I'm sorry, David. I can't."

"Think about it."

"No. I have a lot of work to do tonight."

"Seems like old times," I said. "Goodbye."

12

Teasing Reality with a Redheaded Nude

A few days later, Gloria called.

"What are you doing Thursday?"

"The usual. In the morning, a chukker or two of polo at the club. Then lunch with the Prime Minister of Canada. In the evening, I'll be the keynote speaker at a dinner for retired violists. Poor bastards. They're always playing second fiddle."

"In other words, you don't have any plans."

"Right."

"Good. We're going to the Museum of Modern Art. I'm a member."

"Of course."

"So I can get you in for five bucks."

"Will wonders never cease?"

"This will be kind of an ego trip for me."

"What else is new?"

"I'm featured in one of the exhibits."

"*Lesbians I Have Known and Loved?*"

"I'm not kidding. Have you ever heard of Donna Kelly?"

"I don't think so."

"She made a small splash in the Fifties, but she didn't play the gallery game well enough. Didn't kiss the right asses. So critics and collectors never paid much attention to her. She died a few years ago."

"And now they're starting to appreciate her. Maybe there's hope for me. All I have to do is die."

"Don't count on it."

"They're showing her work at MoMA?"

"Yes. I caught the preview the other night. And five of her paintings are portraits of" (dramatic pause) "yours truly."

"You were really making the rounds, huh? Playwrights. Painters."

"I just modeled for her. She was a little too butch for me."

"How old were you at the time?"

"Twenty. Twenty-one."

"Are you recognizable? Or are both of your eyes on the same side of your nose?"

"No, no. She sampled a lot of styles, but most of her work isn't abstract. You'll see."

"I guess I will."

"And we'll have lunch at MoMA, too. My treat."

"I feel like a kept man. It's a nice feeling."

"I'll check the train schedule. Let you know what time I'll pick you up."

"Okay. But please don't bring me flowers."

"I promise."

"If you think that you have to get me *something*. Well . . . A box of candy. A subscription to *Playboy*."

"Dream on."

It was 11 am when we arrived at the Museum of Modern Art. The new MoMA, just expanded and rebuilt.

At first, I didn't like what they'd done to the *old* MoMA. Too much empty space. Walls too big. Ceilings too high. It seemed chilly and empty. But it was growing on me.

"I remember coming here when I was in college," I told Gloria. "The museum was much smaller then. More intimate. It shared the block with the Whitney, which had an entrance on 54th. They were back-to-back and you could go from one to the other without going outside."

"Memories, memories. Now tell me about the day you met Herbert Hoover."

"Later. If you treat me right."

We escalatored up to the Sixth Floor. To the special exhibit: "Donna Kelly—*Teasing Reality.*"

Gloria smiled.

"When they asked Donna why she painted, she always said, 'I'm teasing reality'."

"Nice phrase."

"You'll see. It's right on target."

I liked most of Donna Kelly's paintings. And her own description of her style was perfect. The images of people and places were real, but never photographic. The brushstrokes were heavy. The paint was thick, textured, bulging off the canvas. You could almost see Donna Kelly's hand piling it on. The colors were vivid, harsh, energetic. Real, but not quite.

"There I am, I am, I am," Gloria said, steering me toward a wall where five paintings were grouped together: "Redhead #1," "Redhead #2," up to "Redhead #5."

Five nudes in a variety of settings: reclining on a boldly checkered couch, walking along a flower-bordered garden path, coquettishly shielding her face with an oriental fan, looking back over her shoulder through an open window at someone or something outside, cradling a Siamese cat in a room filled with *chinoiserie*. Each a study in contrasting patterns and textures, with the same Redhead as the focal point.

Gloria looked around furtively, immodestly, as if she expected the museum-goers to recognize her and ask for autographs. They didn't.

"They're beautiful," I said.

"They?"

"You're beautiful."

Gloria is beautiful, but the painted younger version of her was beautiful in a different way. Still not damaged by disappointment. By love turned cold. Or sour. By hopes unfulfilled.

"That's not the way I wanted her to paint me. I asked her to make my breasts bigger and my butt smaller. She wouldn't."

"She knew what she was doing. I might have erased the flaws. Softened the edges. And I never would have caught that look in your eyes. Defiant. Expectant."

"I didn't like these pictures when I first saw them."

"And now?"

"I wish I could be that girl again."

"For as long as these paintings last, you will be."

Gloria smiled.

"Thank you, David," she said, and kissed me on the cheek.

🍁

We had lunch in the museum at a restaurant they call The Modern. A little snooty for me, but I can be a snob when that's required. In fact, I rather enjoy it. Especially when someone else is picking up the tab.

Gloria ordered a bottle of Cabernet, which we lingered over after a tasty but insubstantial meal. I let the wine relax me.

"Now you've seen me naked," she said.

"I may begin to take you for granted."

She touched the rim of her wine glass lightly. Watched her fingertip caress it.

"It's a strange thing to see yourself that way," she said.

"Naked? In my case, *strange* is an understatement."

"No. I mean the way someone else sees you."

"There are so many someone else's. Even in your own family. I was a son, a brother, a husband, a father."

"We've never talked about your children."

I had wanted to share August tenth with Mandy. If I couldn't do that . . .

I took out my wallet, opened it, showed Gloria the family photograph. She looked at it, looked at me.

"Very attractive group. Even you were kind of cute. All that hair!"

I laughed.

"I guess this is Wife Number Two."

"Yes. Mandy. Our son, Philip. Our daughter, Lisa."

"Do your children live in Connecticut?"

"Philip lives in Greenwich. He's married. Has two kids. Lisa died when . . ."

I wasn't able to finish the sentence. There were tears in my eyes. I hadn't expected that.

Gloria looked away from me, down at the picture.

I rubbed the tears away. Cleared my throat.

"In this photo, she was fifteen."

Gloria nodded.

"You can see the way we're posed. Lisa at the center. She was always at the center."

Gloria waited for me to continue.

"She was a good kid. Bright and gentle. She wrote very well. We thought she was a very promising talent. You know when they say someone's heart is in the right place? That was Lisa. You had to love her. You had no choice."

I touched my chest.

"But her heart was also in the wrong place. On the right side, not the left."

"That's a problem?"

"Sometimes it is. There are twins who are mirror images of each other. One has his heart on the left side, the other on the right. And all the other organs are reversed like that. That's no problem. But it was just Lisa's heart that was in the wrong place. And in that case, there are usually other issues. There were."

I drank some wine. Gloria gave me back my wallet, still open to the family picture.

"When she was very young, it wasn't bad. Maybe she got tired a little quicker than other kids. But as she got older, things got worse. She couldn't exercise much. Had pains in her chest. Shortness of breath. The valves in her heart weren't working right. By the time she was in her teens, she was taking a bunch of different medicines. Blood thinners. Water pills. And she couldn't really live like a kid."

"That's a raw deal."

"She kept getting weaker. Finally, when she was eighteen, she had to have a heart transplant. She got one. But they couldn't find a real match. A right-handed heart. So it didn't work."

Again my vision blurred with tears.

"We lost her a long time ago. Twelve years. But whenever I think about her, it's like it happened yesterday."

"At least you had your son."

"Did we? You know, when I was growing up, my older sister got most of the attention from my parents. She was the wild one. And I was the good one. But I got lost in the shuffle. The same thing happened to Philip. He was two years older than Lisa. Smart. Handsome. But she needed so much from us, we didn't have a lot left over for him. He loved her, too. But he couldn't help resenting her. And us. He's not close to either of us."

I smiled. "Even when we outgrow our parents, we end up repeating their mistakes."

I put my wallet back in my pocket. Poured the last of the Cabernet into Gloria's glass.

"That song I played for you. *My Garden*. I wrote that for Lisa. Just before the operation."

Gloria nodded.

"I never wrote another song."

November 3, 1995
Hail and Farewell

Daniel's 1995 had been an unpleasant year. Nothing dramatic. Just more of the same. At home. At work. Routines. Rituals. No peaks or valleys. A desert road stretching straight ahead, flat, monotonous, monochromatic.

The world at large seemed worse. Massacres in Rwanda and savagery in the Balkans. Assassination in the Middle East and terror in Oklahoma City. Endless tabloid takes on O.J. And Clinton at war with the not-so-Grand Old Party.

Was it really a worse year than any other? Maybe he just wanted it to be.

···

It was Friday afternoon. Daniel was in Eli Fowler's office. Time to plan Eli's traditional end-of-the-year remarks to the management team. A very nervous management team: in January, *aXcess* had been acquired by *Elektra Enterprises*, a Stockholm-based electronics firm. The future had become a question mark.

Eli, approaching age 65, would have to retire next year. The corporate by-laws demanded it.

This would be his farewell address.

Daniel thought, *How about keeping it simple? "I'm incredibly rich. You're not. Hope you find another job. Goodbye."*

Eli had aged well. He was still agile, quietly aggressive, dark-haired (a dye job, of course), almost boyish in a vulgar way. Still abusive with inferiors. The class bully.

"They're worried," Daniel said. "What's *Elektra* going to do to them when you leave?"

"What the hell are they bitching about? They'll get their severance pay. And the job market is good."

He smiled, not at Daniel, but at the third person in the meeting: Gina Braverman-Boone, a thirtysomething athletic blonde, who had joined the company two years ago from a P.R. agency to play a new role: assistant vice president-Office of the Chairman. Eli's sidekick. His hatchetman. His secret sharer.

She was the insider. Daniel had been the insider with Tyler Flint. But never with Eli. Daniel didn't care.

He had nothing at stake. Financially, he was set. Stock-option bonuses for the past twenty years. Four stock splits. A buy-out of his *aXcess* shares by *Elektra* at a premium. And a steadily growing 401-K portfolio.

He supervised an Executive Communications staff of three writers. Speeches, annual reports, annual meetings—they all came out of his shop. He delegated but kept a close watch. He filtered everything they did, tweaked it, revised it, whatever it needed.

By now, he was running on automatic pilot. And on empty. He would leave when Eli retired. Ahead of the purge.

Leave for what?

"This has to be our best holiday party ever," Eli said.

"It will be," Gina said.

Her eyes were stormcloud grey. Her voice was low-pitched, clear, intense. A verbal scalpel.

"She's handling the arrangements," Eli said to Daniel.

No shit.

"I'm working directly with the Plaza staff," she said. "No middle men. Food, drinks, entertainment, decor. The best ever."

She and Eli shared one of their intimate smiles.

He wondered how intimate they were. They were both married. To Daniel, Eli had always seemed sexless. Power was his turn-on. But maybe he was just discrete. And to Gina Braverman-Boone's hyphenated generation, sex was commonplace, almost trivial. Take it wherever you find it, where it can do you the most good.

"And Mr. Berman, I also want my remarks to be the best ever."

"How about *Hail and farewell*?" Daniel asked.

"Too short," Eli said.

He and Gina laughed. Daniel smiled.

"This is the perfect time for a retrospective," Daniel said. "Building a major business for the past quarter century. Some early history. Discoveries at the Tower. Financial growth. Expansion into consumer electronics. Strategy. Tactics. The works."

"Keep it focused on Eli," Gina warned.

"Right," Daniel said.

The sole survivor.

Eli, Virgil Prince and Tyler had owned the only voting shares of *aXcess*. The rest of the stock was voteless, powerless, paid no dividends, but the market price continued to grow.

Eli knew that the party couldn't last forever. He knew how he wanted it to end: on his terms.

Virgil Prince's departure was the beginning of that end. He left in 1978, less than ten years after *aXcess* went public. He was bored. Same old, same old. He needed a new challenge. A new venture. There was already a crew of ambitious young researchers at the Tower, who had become *aXcess's* idea men.

Virgil wanted to start fresh. He wasn't sure what he wanted to do, but he wanted out.

Eli bought all of Virgil's shares. Before Tyler knew Virgil was leaving. After all, what are friends for?

Tyler didn't have a prayer. Eli had stacked the Board of Directors with his buddies. He was on several of their boards. (Together they served a common goal: "You approve my compensation plan and I'll approve yours.") Whenever bonus time rolled around, the Board granted Eli (the mighty CEO) more class A (voting) stock than Tyler (the lowly CFO). Eli's majority share kept swelling. Tyler's minority share never caught up.

In 1985, Tyler left the business to start an investment consulting firm.

Eli had doled out a handful of class A shares to some of the Board members. But now he was king of the hill.

"I'll mention Virgil and Tyler, but only in passing," Daniel said.

Gina pursed her lips and watched him, a young mongoose appraising a weary old snake.

After Tyler left, Eli had begun preparing, slowly, patiently, for the eventual sale of the company. When he was ready to leave. When the price was high enough. When he could shape the right kind of agreement with the chairman of *Elektra*. Who happened to be on the *aXcess* Board.

"I'll have a draft for you the middle of next week," Daniel said.

"Run it by Gina, first."

The mongoose smiled. At Eli.

"Okay," Daniel said.

■■■

Back in his own office, Daniel watched a dreary, wintry Manhattan nightfall.

There was a time when he enjoyed the busy view from his eighth-floor corner window, north along Fifth Avenue, Central Park to the west. Now the view was flat. Cold. He watched people, cars, buses, the way he would watch an ant-farm's primitive, mindless traffic. He could see himself out there, year after year, scurrying to keep up with the parade. Never quite catching up. Never quite falling behind.

A month ago, he had celebrated his fifty-sixth birthday. Alone. Amy was prepping for a major case. She had to stay in New York. She called. Left a card. Their son Tom, in graduate school at Stanford, called. Sent a card.

Daniel had a birthday dinner of lasagna and garlic bread (a takeout from *Mama Vitali's Ristorante* a couple of blocks from the Fairfield station), several glasses of wine, coffee and a chocolate chip cookie. He sang "Happy Birthday to me." Watched *Warlock*, his favorite Western movie, on HBO. Then he went to sleep.

He dreamed he was on the witness stand, testifying on behalf of one of Amy's clients at a big trial. Amy was questioning Daniel and he kept unintentionally messing up his testimony. She was frustrated, furious. The judge and jury were laughing at him. And at Amy. Suddenly she had a gun in her hand. She shot the judge, who continued to laugh. She leaned toward Daniel, whispered, "You'll never get it right," and shot herself. He woke up. Got out of bed. Urinated. Went back to sleep.

Happy Birthday to me.

■■■

His phone rang, pulling him back to the present. It was Ron Berliner, an old friend and classmate at NYU. They had worked together at *TV Guide* for a few years. Then went their separate ways. Now Ron was editing two men's magazines.

"How's it going, Danny?"

"It's going."

"You don't sound too upbeat. Are you free for dinner tonight? Lois is at her mother's for the weekend."

"It's tempting. But it's been a long day."

"And there's your Friday night ritual, of course. Chinese take-out with Amy. God forbid you should break the pattern."

"It's not much of a pattern any more. I mean, I have to call her. Find out if she's coming home. That's probably what we'll do, but . . ."

"I saw her name in the *Times* business section yesterday. A software piracy case."

"Yeah. She's bigger than life," Daniel said.

"Very impressive."

"My picture was in the *Times* once. About ten years ago. I was photographed with three other people from the company. All of us were working at home one day a week. Telecommuting. That was a big deal back then."

"So you were a star, too."

"But the caption was wrong. I became Marketing Assistant Lester McNally. And Lester became me."

"Fifteen minutes of fame, and you screw it up," Ron laughed.

"Count on it. How's the book coming?"

"It isn't. I'll never finish the fucking thing."

"Don't give up. One of us has to write a novel. And it's not going to be me."

"I don't have the time. Or the energy," he said.

"Take more vitamins."

"You know what the problem is, Danny? I've been working on this book for too long. Almost eight years. I don't have the same point of view in my fifties that I had when I was in my forties. I've changed, thank God. So the story keeps changing. The characters keep changing."

"Write faster."

"Brilliant advice. So you're sure about tonight? You want to check with Amy and call me back?"

"Either way, I'm just not in the mood tonight."

"That's what Lois always says."

"Say goodbye, Ron."

"Goodbye, Ron."

He sat watching the relentless ant-farm traffic. Listening to the harsh music of the city: engines growling, horns and sirens wailing, the murmur of a thousand faraway voices.

It was getting late. He should call Amy. He looked at the phone as if it had just said, "You'll never get it right."

He dialed her office number. Her executive assistant answered.

"Hi, Margaret. It's Daniel. Is my wife reachable?"

After almost two minutes on *Hold*, she was.

Her "Hello" was half-hearted: her mind was elsewhere.

"Will you be home for dinner?"

"Eight. Eight-thirty."

"Sesame chicken?"

"Fine. I'll call you if I get stuck."

"See you later."

He returned the phone to its cradle.

He looked past the city's streets at the clear, black sky. Handfuls of stars.

Is there life out there? A better world maybe? Or is someone on that world looking at the stars, too, wondering the same thing?

■■■

At home, Daniel sat in the family room, trying to listen to Mozart and downing his second Manhattan. He poured a third.

The room was too big. The house was too big. Family size. Too many echoes.

He waited for Amy, knowing that when she arrived, the house would seem emptier.

Jacqueline had died almost two years ago. Her last year, her eighteenth, was the worst of their lives. Jacky couldn't ignore the approaching darkness any more. Couldn't smile. Couldn't hope.

She had been brave for so long. From the time she was little.

At first, after she was gone, the three of them seemed closer. Not for long.

Maybe Tom thought his time had finally come. But, unrelentingly, Jacky still dominated their lives. Still kept him in the background.

One day Tom said, "I've been accepted by Stanford graduate school. With a fellowship. I'll be leaving in a few months."

They congratulated him.

"Now you can spend all of your time mourning her," he said.

They protested. They knew he was right. They knew he would probably never live with them again.

For Amy and Daniel, the mourning gradually became something else. Instead of comforting each other, they began to turn away from each other. They worked longer hours. Brought work home. Spent less time together. Went to dinner or the theatre with other couples, instead of just with each other, which used to be what they preferred.

They lived together now like roommates. Casual friends. Sometimes sharing ideas, thoughts. Never sharing feelings.

They weren't sure they still loved each other. They knew they didn't desire each other. They went to bed only to sleep.

And they didn't sleep well.

■■■

Amy arrived home at 8:15. She changed into pajamas and a bathrobe and joined him in the family room. She was exhausted.

Daniel poured her a Manhattan.

"Rough day?" he asked.

"The usual."

"Eli's gearing up for his swan song."

"He's had a pretty good ride."

"Yeah. He's a clever son of a bitch."

"You did pretty well, too."

"I guess so."

"Do you still plan to leave when he does?" she asked matter-of-factly, tightening the belt of her robe.

"Yes."

"What will you do?"

"Write. Consult. Maybe both. Maybe neither. I'm not sure. I haven't thought about it much."

"Don't you care about what you do?"

Her voice registered mild concern.

"Not really."

Amy shook her head. "You never enjoyed your job, did you?"

"I did. In the beginning. But I wasn't a big success like you."

"You did all right."

"You did a hell of a lot better."

Amy shrugged. "Is there anything wrong with being successful?"

"No. Of course not."

"I worked hard."

Daniel smiled. "Eli once said to me that hard work, doing a good job, had nothing to do with success. He should know. He was an operator. He knew how to rig the game."

"Do you think that's what I did?"

"No. You're not in a business I understand. But in my company I saw a lot of turkeys turn into eagles, and some of them didn't know shit from shinola. But they knew the right people."

"So did you. You should have been more aggressive."

"Please. I had a father. I don't need another one."

"You never blame yourself for anything."

"And you're always very forgiving about your own weaknesses. But never about mine."

Neither of them was angry. It was too late for anger.

He emptied the cocktail shaker, refilling her drink and his.

"I wonder what it would have been like for us if Jacky had lived," she said.

"That's too big an 'if'."

"I don't feel things the way I used to."

"You still love your work."

"Do I have anything else to love? Of course, I do. My husband. My son." Her eyes filled with tears. "But I can't feel that any more."

"I can't either."

"We should have listened to Dr. Reiss. After Tom was born, he warned me."

"He didn't say you shouldn't have another baby."

"I had a bad pregnancy. We were lucky that Tom survived. I shouldn't have pushed our luck."

"He turned out to be a strong, healthy kid. There was no way to predict what happened to Jacky."

"I should have known."

Daniel shook his head. "You want to blame someone? My mother had a heart attack. My grandfather, too. It was bad genes. My genes."

"Was there anything else we could do?"

"Nothing."

They didn't comfort each other. She wiped the tears away. They sat in silence for a few minutes.

She yawned, stretched.

"Would you warm up dinner for us?" she asked.

"Sure. I'm great at that."

"It takes talent."

"If you say so. I'll make tea, too."

Fifteen minutes later, they were sitting at the kitchen table, chopsticks in hand, scooping up chicken chunks and rice, washing the food down with hot tea. The Friday night ritual.

Halfway through the meal, Amy said, "There's something we should talk about."

"Lots of things."

"One thing in particular."

When he looked at her, her face reminded him of Ginnie's when she told him she wanted a divorce. Tender, discouraged. He wasn't surprised at what Amy said.

"We should consider separating. For a while."

He nodded.

"I've been looking for an apartment in the city," she said. "The firm will underwrite most of the cost. You could stay here."

"I could."

"If that's all right with you."

"It's all right."

"We'll take it a step at a time. See how things work out."

"Fine."

"For a while."

"I'll call Tom tomorrow," he said.

"I can do that, if you want me to."

"Does it matter who calls him?"

"No."

"Do you want more rice?"

"You can finish it."

"Thanks."

"I'm really tired," she said. "I can't eat any more."

"Why don't you go to sleep? I'll clean up."

Amy walked over to Daniel and kissed him on the forehead.

"Goodnight, Dan."

"Goodnight."

He sat at the kitchen table and watched the second hand of the clock on the wall. Imagined it moving in reverse, pulling him back through time, through thousands of sunrises, sunsets.

He smiled.

"*Maya krasivaya dyevushka*," he whispered. "My beautiful girl."

13

Second Chances

Late one night in August, Gloria phoned me.

"I thought you were staying on Long Island for a couple of weeks," I said.

"So did I. But I got a call today from my mother's attorney. He's an old friend of the family. He says she's going downhill fast. He thinks I should say goodbye."

"Sorry to hear that."

"I'm back in Southport. I'll be driving up to Boston tomorrow morning."

She paused. For her, it was an unusual pause, as if she couldn't find the right words.

"Would you do me a favor?" she said. "A big favor?"

"If I can."

"Come with me."

"To Boston?"

"Yes."

"I'm not sure I understand what you're asking me."

"I don't want to see her alone."

"I don't know . . . "

"You don't have to do anything. Or say anything."

"Who am I supposed to be? The Ghost of Christmas Past?"

"This is not something I want to do. I haven't seen my mother in more than a year. I told you, we've never been close."

"What has that got to do with me?"

"David. Please. I need you to be there. If you're there, it'll be easier for me."

"And what about her? How is she going to feel? She's dying. And her daughter arrives at her bedside with some old fart she's never seen before. Think about it."

"Believe me, I've thought about it."

"I don't know."

"Unless you go with me, I probably won't go."

"Now *I'm* the guilty party."

"No, David. That's my job."

"We would drive up in the morning and come back the same day, right?"

"Right."

"Where in Boston does she live?"

"In one of those big, gloomy apartment buildings on Commonwealth Avenue. My old homestead. I grew up there. Ten rooms with live-in help."

"The silverspoon baby."

"That's me."

"Spoiled rotten."

"But what a wonderful human being I turned out to be."

I laughed. "I don't know why I'm doing this."

"You're my friend. That's a good reason."

"I suppose so."

"I'll pick you up at ten o'clock."

🍁

Have I mentioned the fact that Gloria is an aggressive driver? No surprise there.

On the Connecticut Turnpike on our way to Boston, she took particular pleasure in passing trucks and then cutting them off, smiling maliciously at the teamster in her rear-view mirror. Of course, I knew that if one of these gentlemen decided to track us down and wreak vengeance, I'd be the one to buy the farm. ("I'm sure the old bastard put her up to it.")

When we reached I-84, there was very little traffic and I began to relax.

"So you grew up in Boston," I said. "You don't have the accent."

"You mean: pahk the cah in the Hahvahd yahd? No, thanks. No accents for me."

"Everybody's so mobile these days. Accents are disappearing."

"I was all over the map, too. We lived in France for a couple of years. Went there when I was ten."

"Paris?"

"Yes. We had an apartment not far from the Bois de Boulogne. And we spent summers in Aix-en-Provence."

"Sounds just like my childhood."

"My father had invested in a French start-up company. He went over to make sure they knew what they were doing."

"Did they?"

"With a little coaching."

Gloria's world sounded like a novel by F. Scott Fitzgerald. I felt as if I hadn't lived at all.

"By the time we came back, I could speak French, loved wine and cheese . . ."

"You started hitting the bottle early, huh?"

"A couple of years later, I was whisked off to Washington, Connecticut. To Wyckham Academy, an all-girl school."

"All girls? You were already headed that way."

Gloria laughed. "I told you: when I was a kid, I was straight. But I didn't like it at Wyckham. Too uppity. I had only one friend. We used to speak French to each other."

"Wasn't that a little uppity?"

"*Touché*," she winced. "A few years later I was off to college."

"The Sorbonne?"

"Bryn Mawr. Which was, by the way, the first college in this country to offer graduate degrees to women."

I groaned. "The beginning of the end for the American male."

"But I was still on the go. I got my M.A. at the University of Chicago."

"What did you major in?"

"French."

"Of course."

"Never got a PhD."

"You didn't miss anything."

"Doctor Berger, is it?"

"You may kiss my ring."

"Do you mind if I call you Doc?"

"Yes, I do mind."

A half hour later, we reached the Massachusetts Turnpike, the last leg of the trip. The speed limit went up. Gloria slowed down.

I tried to distract her.

"You remind me of a night—just one night—I spent in a very big, very old apartment house on Park Avenue. Job-related. I worked for an electronics company. We made components for computers, TV sets, sound systems. But we were always working behind the scenes. Known by the industry, not by the public. One day, my boss, the P.R. vice president, has a brainstorm. We'll start an ad campaign. You know: 'If you're watching television, logging onto your computer, listening to your favorite album— you couldn't do it without us.' Not a bad idea. He figured it would help increase our visibility. And our stock price."

"Sounds reasonable."

"So he sent me out with a camera crew to shoot footage of our factories. Our high-tech production lines. Leading edge stuff we could use in TV commercials. We hired a director who was a real character. Harrigan was his name. He looked like a Marine drill sergeant. Crew cut. Permanent frown. Big, bulky guy. When he came to a meeting, he would ball up his trench coat and throw it in the corner."

"Why?"

"I was afraid to ask him."

She laughed.

"We shot some great footage. We didn't actually produce the TV spots, but we edited segments that could be dropped into a forty-second time slot in each of them. We finished late one night. I was going to stay at a hotel. Harrigan wouldn't hear of it. He said we could stay at Grandma's."

"His grandmother's?"

"Actually, she was his mother-in-law. His kids' Grandma. She was a widow. Her husband had been a big shot with the Metropolitan Opera or the Philharmonic. I forget which. She lived alone on Park Avenue, in an ancient building. She had lived there for fifty years. A huge apartment. Lots of spare bedrooms, Harrigan said."

"Sounds familiar."

"The place was patrolled by a platoon of doormen, elevator men, security guards. Most of them looked as old as the building. Down in the lobby, there was a big beam that came down to lock the front door. It was like the village gate in *King Kong*."

She laughed.

"They knew Harrigan. Otherwise we probably would have been shot on the spot. So we went upstairs and I met Grandma. A nice, dignified lady in her eighties. Harrigan showed me around the apartment. There was a bedroom for each of her four grandchildren. And every bedroom had pictures of that kid with his or her parents and grandparents. And a closetful of his or her clothes. I was assigned to one of these rooms. Harrigan showed me where the kitchen was, in case I got hungry."

"Boston, twenty miles," she said. Her hands gripped the steering wheel a little tighter.

"I couldn't fall asleep. I was thirsty, so I went to the kitchen. The apartment was very creepy."

I was exaggerating, but I wanted to entertain Gloria. Calm her down.

"There were these high ceilings with fancy carved molding. Antique furniture with cherubs and claws. Lots of empty rooms. It was very dark. And the floor creaked. I found a glass in one of the kitchen cabinets, orange juice in the refrigerator. I sat at the table and was drinking the juice when the cupboard started to move. This big, double-doored cupboard was pushing out of the wall, turning toward me! What the hell was going on? Was I dreaming? It was like I was in a horror movie. I expected Dracula or the Wolfman to jump out and grab me."

"Which one was it?"

"It was the maid. She apparently lived in a room behind the cupboard. She had heard me moving around and she was checking to see who it was."

Gloria didn't laugh.

"We're almost there," she said.

There was nothing gloomy about the apartment house where Gloria's mother lived.

The doorman said, "Miss Mundy. Nice to see you."

"Thank you, Robert. Nice to see you, too."

Robert followed us into the lobby, picked up the phone and dialed it.

As we approached the elevator, he said, "Flora? This is Robert. Please tell Mrs. Mundy that her daughter is on the way up. Thank you."

In the elevator, Gloria said, "Flora has been with my mother for thirty years. Since we came back from Paris. Mom is totally dependent on her. Always has been."

When we reached her mother's apartment, the door was open. A tall black woman was standing in the doorway. She was slim, handsome, wearing a long, dark brown dress.

"Good morning, Gloria. How are you?"

Her smile was formal, dignified. Her hands were clasped in front of her, as if we had just interrupted her prayers.

"I'm fine, Flora. How are you?"

"Very well, thank you." She unclasped her hands, held them out palms up. "I wish I could say the same for your mother. I'm so glad you're here."

She closed the door behind us. Walked into the apartment with Gloria, ahead of me.

Flora carried herself the way the mistress of the house would. Gloria let her take the lead.

"The nurse is having lunch in the kitchen. She's here around the clock. I thought you'd want to be alone with your mother."

"Yes, I do."

I felt totally out of place. Out of synch.

The air in the apartment was heavy and stale, as if the windows were never opened. And there was a trace of a medicinal aroma.

When they reached a door at the far end of the apartment, Flora stopped and opened it.

"She may be asleep, but you can wake her," Flora said.

Gloria turned around and said, "Come with me, David," and entered her mother's bedroom. I was a couple of steps behind her.

Her mother was asleep. A frail-looking, gray-haired woman. Slim and small, she was freckled like her daughter. She must have been a redhead.

Gloria looked down at her mother for a minute or two. Flora remained in the hall just outside the door, watching Gloria.

"Mom. Mom."

Gloria touched her arm gently. Shook it gently.

Her mother's eyes opened, saw Gloria, then closed for a moment.

Resolutely, the old woman opened them again and looked at Gloria. Without warmth.

"I was wondering if you'd come," she said.

"How are you, Mother?"

"I'm dying. That's why you're here, isn't it?"

"I thought I'd . . . "

"If you're wondering, I'm not afraid," her mother said. "Living is overrated."

She looked at me.

"Who's he? Not your boyfriend, I hope. He's old enough to be your father. Not handsome enough. Old enough."

"He's a friend."

Her mother laughed, an angry, brittle laugh. "I thought all your *friends* were women. You know what I mean?"

"I know what you mean."

"I'll never understand that."

"Mom, it doesn't matter. I didn't come here to talk about that."

"Why did you come here? To make sure that I was dying?"

"Please, don't . . . "

Her mother seemed too weak to move. But her eyes glowed with anger, resentment.

"I made out my will a couple of years ago," she said. "Left everything to the Cancer Society. Nothing to you. Nothing."

"That's a good idea."

"Your Daddy left you with plenty, didn't he?"

"Mom . . . "

"Didn't he?"

"Yes."

"His wonderful little girl." She looked at me. "My husband was quite a charmer. He made a fortune and lived the high life. He loved the ladies. He worshipped his wonderful little girl and tolerated his wife."

"Mother."

Her mother continued to speak to me. "When Gloria was five or six, I realized she would always be Daddy's little girl. Never mine. So I told him I wanted another baby. I pleaded with him. A child for me. Someone who would love me. He said, No. He would never divorce me. Would always take

117

care of me. What was his was his. But no more sex. No more children. And that was that."

Gloria clenched her fists. Said nothing.

"But I was sure I would have a second chance. When Gloria had children." She looked at Gloria. "Do you know what grandchildren are? A second chance to be loved." She looked at me again. "But Gloria wasn't interested in men. Or children. No second chances. No husband. No daughter. No grandchildren."

"I didn't come here to argue."

"There's nothing to argue about. Do you want me to forgive you?" Her mother smiled.

"No. I just want. . . I don't know what I want."

"I know what I want. Not to see you again."

She turned away from us. Looked at a faded still-life painting on the bedroom wall.

Gloria watched her for a minute or two. She turned and looked at me. Her eyes were vacant, lifeless.

"Let's go," she said.

Flora followed us to the front door. She didn't say goodbye.

Neither did Gloria.

May 12, 1980
Eulogies

On the Thursday night Amy called to tell him that his father had died, Daniel was in a hotel room in San Francisco. He was watching a TV program celebrating the *Miracle on Ice*—the recent Winter Olympics victory of the U.S. hockey team. The program's message: President Carter should reverse his decision to boycott the Moscow Summer Olympics. He wasn't being fair to American athletes.

As if boycotting the Olympics will stop the Russians from fighting in Afghanistan.

Beyond the U.S. hockey team, there wasn't much to celebrate in 1980. Interest rates over twenty percent. A bungled rescue mission failing to free the American hostages in Iran. A soon-to-be-departed President who warned of the malaise that he seemed to generate.

Daniel had accompanied Eli Fowler and Tyler Flint to a series of meetings with investors and securities analysts in three cities: San Diego, Los Angeles, San Francisco. He was flying home on Friday morning.

Amy said the funeral was Sunday. He didn't have to worry: Carol had made all the arrangements.

His father's death was not a surprise. He had fought against a rapidly spreading cancer for almost a year.

And, of course, he died when I was out of town. His parting gesture.

···

He and Carol were meeting with Rabbi Singer at the funeral parlor, a few minutes before the ceremony.

Daniel was trying to pay attention to the rabbi, but he couldn't focus on the words. His attention kept drifting. And he was annoyed by that peculiar intonation all rabbis have, whether or not they are foreign-born.

They must teach that accent at the Yeshiva. The way they teach doctors to scribble prescriptions. And pharmacists to decipher the scribble.

"As we agreed, it will be a brief, simple service. I'll begin with two of the Psalms. Then the *El Maleh Rachamim*. And the *Kaddish*. I'll say a few words about your father, and then who should I introduce?"

"We'd like Stephen, my son, to speak first," Carol said.

"He's how old now?"

"Seventeen."

The rabbi smiled proudly, as if reaching that age was an exceptional accomplishment.

"Then I'll speak," Carol said. "And Daniel will follow me."

The rabbi looked at Carol and Daniel in turn.

"Your father was a fine man. Intelligent, a scholar. He had a good heart. I know he was a great asset to his family as he was to our Temple."

Carol smiled. Daniel nodded.

The rabbi looked at his watch. "We'll begin in a few minutes."

The reception area was noisy and crowded. Daniel and Carol rejoined Amy and Jon and Stephen.

"You'll be speaking first," Carol said to Stephen.

He was a tall, handsome teenager. Outgoing. Confident.

"I'm ready," he said.

"Great turnout," Jon said.

Daniel reached into his breast pocket and touched the slim, folded sheaf of papers. He had written his eulogy, just to be safe. He'd worked on it carefully and rehearsed it.

For Daniel and Amy, the funeral was not just a reminder of their own mortality. They both kept thinking of Jacqueline, four years old, with a damaged heart that would someday betray her. Already living in a shadow. She was at home with her brother, watched over by the au pair.

"There's Uncle Morris," Carol said and waved.

He was their father's brother. A precise, pedantic professor of philosophy, he had been forced to retire several years early after a severe heart attack. Morris was a bitter, childless man with a wife (Aunt Edith) who seemed to respond to life more philosophically than her husband.

"I never imagined I would outlive him," Uncle Morris said, as if he were making a profound observation.

"It's all a matter of luck," Aunt Edith said, kissing Daniel on the cheek.

"Yeah. Life's a crapshoot," Jon agreed, with the conviction of someone who's lost a bundle at that game.

"How are you feeling, Uncle Morris?" Carol asked.

"I'm hanging on," he answered, sighing.

"Tightly," added Aunt Edith, with a trace of a smile.

"My parents are late, as usual," Amy apologized.

"You know your father always gets lost," Daniel said. "Don't worry."

"I'm surprised he got to work every day."

Daniel liked Amy's father. He was a good-natured, gentle man. A lawyer, too, but not a high flyer like Amy. He had a small-time, local practice. Still kept his hand in. Mortgages, wills. Nuts and bolts. He was very much in awe of his daughter's success.

Her mother was more assertive, more like Amy. She was one of the could-have-beens, should-have-beens. The product of a time when she was discouraged from applying her aggressiveness to a career.

Amy's parents arrived a moment after Rabbi Singer invited the family into the chapel. Amy waved her parents over, kissed them, pulled them along with her.

They sat in the front pew. The closed, shiny wooden coffin waited patiently by the altar for its blanket of earth.

Earlier that morning, there had been a viewing for the family. Daniel wished there hadn't been. His father's face was grotesque. Unreal. A mask of white and pink. Serene where there had rarely been serenity. Forgiving where there had rarely been forgiveness.

"Death be not proud . . ." if this is what you leave behind.

After the other attendees had been seated, Rabbi Singer began the service. He chanted the Hebrew verses skillfully, soulfully, his eyes seeking Daniel's eyes, and Carol's. God's messenger.

Daniel's father could read Hebrew fluently. He not only understood what he was reading, he explained the prayers, analyzed them. But he never said that he believed in God.

"Who knows?" he would say. "God was invented by Man, wasn't He?"

He was one of the officers of the Temple. Eventually President of the Congregation. Served on the Board. Took classes in Hebrew, the Talmud. He taught classes, too. Edited the weekly newsletter. Wrote a humor column in it. Pledged money. Raised money.

But he once said, "If there is a God, why should He care about us? What are we? Little bugs running around in the world, thinking we're big shots? Here for a minute and gone before you know it."

Rabbi Singer led the Mourner's *Kaddish*. Then he smiled at his audience, and raised his eyes to the ceiling as if he could see God just behind the chandelier. He began his eulogy.

"I would like to say a few words about Marvin Berman, a dear friend, a man who gave so much of himself and his talents to his family, his community and his religion. In a short while, we'll hear from some of those closest to him: his son and daughter, and his grandson. But in my own way, I felt as if I was part of Marvin's *extended* family. His *Temple* family.

"When it came to supporting our Temple, Marvin was not one of those people who passed the buck. The buck stopped with him, literally and figuratively. In the literal sense, he was always a generous contributor to our Temple. And nobody was a better fundraiser than he was. I remember when . . ."

Daniel wondered what people would say about him at his funeral. There wouldn't be any heartfelt rabbinical tributes. In a few years, he and Amy would join the Reform Temple in Bridgeport. So they could send their children to Hebrew school. So they could be prepared for their *bar/bat mitzvahs*. You know: tradition.

But Daniel didn't believe in God or heaven or angels or hell. And he couldn't understand why anyone did. What kind of God would create a world as screwed up as this one? Only a God who didn't deserve to be worshiped.

Amy was less affirmative about her atheism, but no less skeptical than Daniel. She said that she sometimes prayed that Jacky would live a long life, but she didn't know who she was praying to. Daniel said he knew: No one.

". . .as I promised. So now I'd like to introduce Marvin Berman's grandson, Stephen Miller, with his memories of his grandfather. Stephen."

Daniel admired Stephen's poise. His performance. He spoke without notes, with a half-smile. Hesitating now and then, as if he was treasuring a memory before he shared it, he watched the reactions of his mother and father. Holding onto the podium and leaning over it to emphasize a point now and then, he showed tears in his eyes, charming his audience. Sincere but, at the same time, enjoying every minute in the spotlight.

"And he would say to me, 'If you don't know a word, look it up. Then it'll be yours forever.' But he didn't have to look *anything* up. Grandpa was the smartest person I ever knew. Probably the smartest person I'll *ever* know.

"And the funniest. Nobody could tell a joke like Grandpa. He could always make you laugh. He once told me the secret of being a great joke teller. Be *serious*."

Several people in the chapel laughed.

"It's true. He said, 'If you're laughing, you spoil other people's fun.' That's what he said."

Then *he* became more serious.

"If I had a problem, or was worried, I could always go to him for advice. After I talked to my mother and father, of course."

Stephen smiled at his parents. Several people grunted their approval.

He's telling the truth. He loved my father. Admired him. But what a showman that kid is.

"I'll always remember him. And I'll always miss him." Pause for a sigh. "Mom."

Carol hugged and kissed Stephen as she passed him. She put a single index card on the podium. Glanced at it occasionally.

"My father and I were very close," she said. "We lived in the same house with him—Jon and Stephen and I—for many years. Shared our lives with him. When my mother died, much too soon, I think that brought us even closer together."

She looked down for a moment. Cleared her throat. She was sweet. She meant every word.

But Daniel remembered the arguments, the shouting, the anger. He and his mother hovering in the background. His father and sister in the arena. Over and over, crowding out all the other memories of his childhood.

Anger is better than indifference, he thought. *At least you're getting a reaction.*

". . .such an important part of our lives. When times were hard, he helped us pull through. With advice, assistance, understanding. Jon and I will always be grateful to him. He did so much for us. And for Stephen."

Daniel began to think about the eulogy he had written. It was well crafted. It had a beginning, a middle and an end. Truthful, as far as it went. It was the best he could do for his father. But it wasn't what Stephen and Carol had done. It couldn't be.

"As my son said, we'll always remember him. And we'll always miss him. Because we'll always love him."

She cried for a moment, dabbed at her eyes with a tissue, swallowed hard and said, "Daniel."

He walked toward the podium, kissing Carol on the cheek as she passed him. Pale, his hands shaking, he turned to face the chapel, took the folded speech out of his pocket, and placed it on the podium. He glanced down at the top page and began.

"Marvin Berman was a tough act to follow." (Scattered laughter.) "He had the remarkable ability to be good at everything he tried. Math? Straight A's. Accounting? Passed the CPA test first time around. Music? Played three instruments after taking only one or two lessons. Writing? Short stories, newspaper columns. Joke-telling? A regular Henny Youngman. Making money? A big success. What's a son to do?" (Smiles. Laughter.)

"I'll tell you what this son did. He learned by example. Tried to do what his father always did and always told him to do: work hard to be the best you can be.

"Of course there were times when we disagreed. That's the way of fathers and sons. But it was amazing how often he turned out to be right. Much as I hated to admit it. As someone once said, 'The older I got, the smarter my father became.' That's also the way of fathers and sons.

"To Marvin Berman, family was everything. That was Rule Number One. You did everything for your family. You . . ."

Daniel suddenly felt a tightness in his throat. His eyes began to fill with tears. He tried to read his script, but he couldn't. He still had two pages to go before he finished.

He tried to look at the faces in the chapel. All he could see was a blur.

He could feel the sympathy in the chapel, the willingness to share his pain. But they didn't understand his pain.

His mother, always out of reach because she couldn't hear him. His father, because he wouldn't hear him.

Daniel was crying because he cared so much. Because he cared so little.

14

Sic Transit Gloria Monday

One morning, about a week after the trip to Boston, I was having breakfast with Morty at The Sailor's Castle.

Barbara and Niki had returned to California.

"I've been a real schmuck," Morty said.

"My sentiments exactly."

"She's quite a lady, isn't she?"

"She is. And your granddaughter is going to be just like her."

"I think so. She's a little doll."

"Yeah. Smart. Pretty. So grown up."

"Thank God they came to see me."

"And now you can return the compliment, right?"

Morty pointed his bagel toward the West Coast. "You bet. We've made plans already. I'm going to visit them in a couple of months."

"Take my advice: don't overdo it. If they're anything like me, it won't take them long to get sick and tired of you."

"Fortunately, they're nothing like you."

I smiled. "I'm glad for you, Morty. Really."

He smiled, too. "Thanks."

"Any big events coming up?"

"No, nothing at the moment. How's your book going?"

"It's too soon to tell. But I think I've made a good start. I'm not sure how to construct it. But I'm working on the pieces, anyway."

"And Gloria? Have you fallen in love with her yet?"

I shook my head. "There you go, schmucking it up again."

"You see her all the time, right?" He leaned forward, his eyes narrowed conspiratorially. "She's young. Beautiful. Successful. Lives in your favorite house. Can love be far behind?"

"Sorry to disappoint you. It's not about love."

"If you say so. But I'll reserve judgment."

As if on cue, a couple of minutes later Gloria Monday came into the store.

Morty said, "We were just talking about you."

"I'm flattered."

"Coffee? Bagels?" I offered.

"No, thanks. I've had breakfast." She looked at me. "I was taking a walk. I thought you might be here. Can I tear you away for a few minutes?"

"Sure. I'd rather be with you than with this old fart."

Morty laughed. "Ingrate."

I left with Gloria.

"In the mood for walking?" she asked.

"Always. How are you feeling?"

"I'm fine."

"Any news? From Boston?"

"She died. Yesterday."

"I'm sorry."

"I wish I could feel less ambivalent. I'm mourning. And I'm not."

"I know what you mean."

"Do you? Or are you just saying that?"

I stopped. Put my hand on her shoulder. She stopped. Turned to look at me.

"I understand," I said.

She studied my face for a moment, found what she was looking for, nodded. We continued to walk.

"I want to thank you again for coming with me," she said.

"You didn't give me much choice."

"I guess not."

"I'm sorry it didn't turn out better for you."

"It was what I expected. No deathbed miracles."

"When is the funeral?"

"Wednesday."

"Do you need me to . . . ?"

She smiled. "No, no, no. Thanks. I'll be fine."

We walked in silence for a minute or two.

"David, there's something else I wanted to tell you."

"Another trip with you?"

"No. But I *am* going to do some traveling. After the funeral."

"Where are you going?"

"To Paris."

"That's a good idea. You could use a vacation."

"It's more than a vacation. I'm going to live there for a while."

"You just moved here. I thought you were settling down."

"I don't settle down."

We had reached a little park by the water, near the yacht club. Seagulls orbited overhead. The grass was soft and damp with morning dew. We could already feel the first taste of August heat. I could already feel the loss of her.

I pointed to one of the benches facing the water. We sat down together.

"Why are you going away?"

"You should know. I'm always on the move."

"What about your house?"

"I've invited a couple of friends to stay there. For as long as I'm gone."

"How long will that be?"

"I have no idea."

She took my hand in hers. "I came to Southport so I could be closer to my mother. But not *very* close. I felt that I owed her something. I thought I would see her a few times before she died. And that would be the end of it."

"So you had always planned to go to Paris."

"No. I'm not a planner. I got a call. Three, four days ago. From a woman who runs a theatrical company there. I've known her for years. She has a wonderful apartment on the *Ile Saint Louis*. Right on the Seine. She just kicked her boyfriend out. For keeps. She invited me to stay with her."

"Sounds charming."

"I've actually done some acting with her company. Small parts. It's lots of fun."

"Maybe you'll be a star someday."

"Never. I'm good at a lot of things. But not that good at any of them."

"Actress. Artist's model. Writer."

She laughed. "You know I'm not much of a writer, either. I wanted to pass along some things. To other women. I've said everything I have to say."

"Maybe you should try fiction."

127

"I wish I could. I'm not creative. Never have been. It's what I admire most. What I'm attracted to most."

"I'll miss you, Gloria."

"I'll miss you, too." She touched my face with her hand. "But we're going to write to each other. Lots of letters. Not emails. Is that a deal?"

"It's a deal."

"And I want you to give me something before I go."

"What do you give a woman who has everything?"

"I want to read your novel."

"It isn't a novel yet. It's fragments. I'm not even sure how I'll put it all together."

"I want to read it. I might remind you that I'm the reason you're writing it."

"You might."

"If it weren't for me, you'd be stuck somewhere in the middle of the First World War. Isn't that true?"

"Yes."

"In other words, I've been your muse. Admit it."

"I admit it."

"Then let me take the memory of your book with me."

I sighed. "You're a hell of a negotiator."

"Does that mean, Yes?"

"Only if you come to my house and read it there. Not a page leaves the premises."

"You've made me a very happy woman."

"That's only because you haven't read it yet."

"Shall we go?" she motioned.

"Now?"

"*Now* is my favorite word."

A half hour later, she was sitting in my living room, the pages of my manuscript in her lap, reading what there was of my novel. I was sitting in the kitchen, drinking coffee, reading *The New York Times*, and feeling sorry for myself.

I was just about to start the crossword puzzle when she came into the kitchen.

She stood in the doorway, opened her arms to me.

"David, come here."

I walked over to her. She embraced me, kissed my cheek lightly, rested her head on my shoulder. I put my arms around her.

It had been a long time since I held a woman close to me. Warmth. Softness. The scent of perfume.

"Thank you, David," she whispered.

"It's only a beginning," I said.

She looked at me affectionately, approvingly. "But it's you. That's what matters. It's you."

Holding her in my arms, feeling her warmth, her approval, I didn't want to let her go.

"After you leave, will I ever see you again?" I asked.

"Of course you will."

But I knew from the sound of her voice, from the look in her eyes, from the way that she lived, that I never would.

15

September Song

Ted Copeland's retirement party was on a Friday evening in the middle of September. His company rented their favorite East Side steak house for the whole night.

At first, I didn't plan to go. To me, corporate parties are like elephants dancing: self-conscious, clumsy, embarrassing to watch.

But Ted told me Mandy and Philip would probably be there. (Philip and Ted's son Barry were friends when they were in their teens and still kept in touch.) So I got all gussied up in a jacket and tie and took the train to New York.

It was a beautiful city night. A perfect blend of summer and fall: clear sky, mild temperature, pleasant breeze. People were smiling. Even the traffic seemed good-natured.

When I reached the restaurant, I was in the mood to keep walking. The way I used to when I was in college and came into Manhattan at night, often alone, but never lonely in the company of thousands of strangers. Tasting the city, feeling the possibilities, stepping out of the moment into another place, another time. Imagining what my life could be. Would be.

Now there was little to imagine. Much to remember. Gloria Monday had started me not only remembering, but shaping those memories. Trying to understand them.

Now Gloria was becoming a memory, too.

The party was well under way when I arrived. A pianist was playing a real piano. Show tunes, standards.

There was an open bar. Knots of executives crowded the room, with a scattering of corporate women, plus wives and husbands. Amid bursts of too-loud laughter, two or three couples were trying to dance in an open space near the piano.

I didn't see Mandy or Philip, so I headed for the bar where I picked up a Manhattan and snared a passing *hors d'oeuvre*. Then I zeroed in on Ted and Elaine. They were standing back to back like a SWAT team at a raid, parrying shots from a passing parade of celebrants.

Ted looked relieved. The day of reckoning was here at last. Elaine looked exhausted. Ready to head for Florida. Her smile was wearing out fast.

I inserted myself into the parade, waited my turn, shook Ted's hand.

"I thought you weren't bailing out until November," I said.

"Actually, it'll be official at the end of October. But I decided to take some vacation, too."

"Ah, the idle rich."

"Idle, yes. Rich, no."

"Your modesty becomes you. Have you . . . "

A chubby young man in a dark suit elbowed me out of the way. One of Ted's Marketing MBAs, I guessed. I could catch up with Ted later. I bowed out gracefully.

"Ted, I've got to tell you," the young man stage whispered, "Gorman is sure as hell getting on my nerves. He told Monty . . . "

Elaine turned, saw me, started to speak, stopped, started again. "David, how've you been?"

I kissed the air near her cheek. "Fine. Big night for both of you."

"Yes. We're ready. Boy, are we ready." She took my arm, pulled me away from the crowd, came closer to me. "I wanted to thank you."

She was uneasy. She had always blamed me for separating from Mandy, never considering that Mandy and I might have reached that decision together.

"For what?"

"The advice you gave Ted. About Barry. You were right. Everything's fine now."

"Glad I could help."

"When you're close to someone, you don't always see things clearly."

"That's only natural."

"Thanks again. We really appreciate it. I really appreciate it."

"Is Barry here?"

She shook her head and smiled. "He's down at Walter Reed. He left this morning to consult on a couple of very serious cases."

I smiled, sharing her pride. She gave my arm a squeeze and went back to her SWAT-team position.

I tried to reach Ted again, but he was trading barbs with a trio of noisy colleagues. He glanced at me, shrugged. I waved and returned to the bar for another Manhattan.

Two pigs-in-a-blanket later, Mandy arrived. Slim. Energetic. Decisive. Beautiful, especially if you go for slim, energetic, decisive women.

I was lurking in a remote corner of the restaurant, enjoying my drink, thankfully unengaged in conversation. Mandy headed for Ted and Elaine. She didn't see me.

I was reminded of all the times I had enjoyed watching her. Even when we were kids. She always held her head high. Challenged you to be smarter or faster or better.

In Junior High and High School, she was my friend, but never my girlfriend. I watched her in a new way, hating the older boys who kissed her or held her hand, who touched her the way I wished I could touch her.

When she became my wife, I would watch her walk into a room and still take pleasure in that. As if it were the first time I had ever seen her.

Tonight, I felt that pleasure.

I waited, a patient voyeur, while she embraced, kissed, conversed with Ted briefly, with Elaine at length.

I remembered. Kisses. Laughter. Passion. Shards of time. The two of us. The four of us. The two of us again, but not the same.

"May I buy you a drink?" I asked.

"Hi, David," she said, and kissed my cheek. "Yes. A Manhattan would be fine."

I wove my way through the crowd, picked up her drink, wove my way back.

"Thanks. Have you seen Philip?"

"He called," Elaine said. "He can't make it tonight. An emergency with one of his clients."

"Do accountants make house calls?" I wondered. "CPA alert! Come quickly! My tax return is running a high fever!"

Mandy laughed. Elaine tried to laugh but she had run out of steam.

"Why don't we let you guys keep meeting and greeting for a while?" I said. "We can hook up with you later."

"Yes. Okay," Elaine said.

"I wrote my own speech for tonight," Ted said.

"Fortunately, most of the people here will be too drunk to remember it," I said.

I led Mandy to my relatively quiet corner of the restaurant.

"I'm sorry Philip won't be here," she said. "I was hoping we could talk. Without the usual crew hovering around him."

"You see him alone sometimes, don't you?"

"Yes. But I never know what to say. I always come up empty. And I'm supposed to be the grown-up," she frowned.

"He's a grown-up, too. He can form complete sentences."

"We did a lousy job with him."

"Among other lousy jobs. Our marriage comes to mind."

Mandy nodded.

The noise level around us was escalating.

"I can hardly hear you," she said.

"Why don't we talk later? I'll walk you home after the party."

She smiled. "Do you want to carry my books?"

I leaned closer to her. "Only if you promise to kiss me good night."

"I'm not promising you anything," she whispered.

The pianist pounded out several loud, attention-getting chords.

"Ladies and gentlemen," a deep male voice said over the public address system. "Ladies and gentlemen. It's time for a little fun. At Ted Copeland's expense, of course!"

Laughter. Applause.

The speaker was Steve Hewitt, Ted's boss, the smug, dapper CEO of the company.

"Ted, my man, come on up here!"

More laughter. More applause.

Ted joined Hewitt on the dais. The pianist began to play *September Song* softly in the background.

"Yes, Ted," Hewitt said, "it's a long, long time from May to December. And you're jumping ship in September—before you've finished next year's marketing plans!"

Laughter.

"Steve, you're on your own," Ted said.

"As if that's anything new!"

Inside jokes. Forced hilarity. Elephants dancing.

When it was Ted's turn, he paid the expected tributes to the company, higher management, his colleagues, his team. A special thank you to his wife.

It was a standard farewell. Despite that, he actually meant it. And he even passed the torch.

"Sam Pinella is rarin' to go as the new Marketing Veepee. Aren't you, Sam?"

"Damn right!" Sam agreed.

"So I'm confident that my team—and my company—are in very good hands. And if you ever need my advice, don't hesitate to call the *El Capitan Country Club* in Sarasota. They'll page me on the golf course. Or in the sauna. Thanks again, one and all, and goodbye."

After another drink or two, a generous sampling of *hors d'oeuvres*, and brief snatches of conversation with the guests of honor, Mandy and I left the party.

The street seemed quiet by comparison.

She lived on East 86th, about a fifteen-minute walk from the restaurant. Fifteen minutes. Enough time for me to begin . . .

To begin what?

"You don't really have to take me home," she said. "This isn't a high-crime area."

"If it was, you might have to protect *me*."

After a moment, she said, "Elaine couldn't wait to leave. She wanted Ted to retire a couple of years ago. She didn't enjoy being a corporate wife."

"And he loved the life."

"He was very good at it."

"You're still not thinking about retiring?" I wondered.

"I would probably miss work. But honestly, I'm not as sure about that as I used to be."

"You should do what I did. You know. Keep your hand in. I did some consulting for five, almost six years, after I retired. Taught a couple of classes in P.R. at Fairfield University. You could teach, too, I'm sure."

"We have connections at Columbia. That's a possibility."

"I even wrote a book or two."

"Finally," she said, and smiled.

"Finally."

"It's something to think about."

The air was becoming a little colder. The breeze a little more aggressive.

"The hardest thing isn't keeping busy," I said, "It's being alone."

She didn't respond.

"Isn't it?" I asked.

"I haven't always been alone."

"I know. Ted keeps me posted."

"You haven't been a monk, either. Elaine keeps me posted."

We both laughed.

"After a while, I got tired of it," I said. "Too much work for too little return. I'll never grow up. I still think sex is better with romance."

"Your fatal flaw."

"Guilty, as charged."

"Then why not look for romance, too?"

"Did you?"

"No."

"I didn't have to look for romance. I'd already found it."

"David . . . "

"I mean it."

"That's three or four Manhattans talking."

"No. It's me talking."

We walked in silence for a minute or two.

"I'm working on a new novel," I said.

"That's good."

"It's about remembering."

"Remembering?"

"That's what people do when they get to be our age."

"Not me. I'd rather not remember."

"Mandy, there was more to our lives than Lisa. Wasn't there?"

"I'm not in the mood for this."

"Okay. But I want to see you again. When you might be in the mood."

"I may never be in the mood."

"I want to see you."

"It doesn't make sense."

"May I call you?"

"All right. You can call me."

We didn't speak again until we reached the apartment building where she lived. We stood at the entrance. The doorman opened the door. Held it open.

"Good night," I said, leaning toward her.

She stepped back, put her hand against my chest.

"No. You can't kiss me," she said, and went inside.

The doorman smiled, as if his team had won.

October 20, 1970
Le Tourbillon de la Vie

It was a cruel year.

Bad vibes everywhere. My Lai. Kent State. The Cambodian "incursion" (a devious synonym for "invasion.").

Idols, kissing each other goodbye. The Beatles. The Supremes. Simon and Garfunkel. Peter, Paul and Mary.

Idols, dying. Jimi Hendrix. Janis Joplin.

Even Daniel Berman, apolitical, concentrating-on-my-career Daniel Berman, felt the bad vibes.

Worst of all, his marriage proposal hung in the air like a love-sick balloon, waiting for Amy to say, "Yes."

When they had started dating, she was uneasy. After all, Daniel was her friend. She'd known him all her life. He was practically her brother.

Gradually, she managed to get over that feeling. She could kiss him. Hold him in her arms. Caress him. Be caressed. Be aroused.

The pleasure they gave each other finally broke down the barriers.

Daniel was almost happy. Almost. He wanted to marry Amy. He asked her. She said, Not yet.

Week after week, month after month, she said, Not yet.

They talked about what they would do *if* they got married.

Where they would live. "Probably Connecticut."

Where they would vacation. "Paris. Venice. Florence."

How many children they would have. "Two. Like the song says, *a girl for you and a boy for me.*"

But week after week, month after month, she said, Not yet.

They went to Broadway, Off-Broadway and Way-Off-Broadway shows. Concerts. Jazz clubs.

Dined, drank and danced at every *in* spot.

Biked in Central Park. Strolled through the Zoo.

Watched Giants games on TV. Knicks games in person.

All the required New York City stuff.

They spent quiet time together, too. At her apartment. At his.

But week after week, month after month, she said, Not yet.

She said, We could live together.

He said, Not until we're married.

She said, You're old fashioned. We both know, marriage is a dying art.

He said, Dying, maybe. But it ain't dead. "Will you marry me?"

She said, "Not yet."

■■■

It was late morning on a crisp, sunny October Sunday. Daniel had slept at Amy's apartment. He had already showered, shaved and dressed. She was in the process.

He was making breakfast. Scrambled eggs, sausages.

"Hurry up," he said. "It'll get cold."

She came into the kitchen in her bathrobe. No make-up. Her hair still wet.

"It's amazing how beautiful you look in the morning," he said.

"You're so full of shit."

"You really know how to take a compliment. Sit down and eat."

"Yes, my lord."

She kissed his mouth. He stroked her wet hair. She sat down. He served breakfast.

"The weather is great today. We should take advantage of it," he said. "A walk in the park. Have lunch, maybe at that Italian place on 63rd."

"Okay."

"And a movie."

"Didn't we just go to the movies?" She frowned. "What was it?"

"*Five Easy Pieces.*"

"Not easy for me. Grim. Tedious."

"Funny, too, sometimes."

"Barely. I didn't care about any of them."

"You're a cold-blooded bastard, Amy."

"Get used to it."

"But you are beautiful in the morning."

"What about at night?"

"Always beautiful."

"I assume you have a particular movie in mind."

"*Jules and Jim.* One of my favorites. It's a revival. An early François Truffaut film. Sixty-one or sixty-two. It's at the Paris."

"I've forgotten most of my French. I hate reading titles."

"Get used to it."

"If I must."

"You probably saw it when it came out."

"Maybe I did," she said. "I don't remember movies. For you, they're like a religion."

"I wouldn't go that far."

She pointed her index finger at his heart. Raised the hammer of her thumb. Made a clicking trigger-sound with her tongue. Down came the hammer-thumb.

"You got me," he groaned.

"I've got you, all right. You're still in love with make-believe. Can't imagine why."

"Reality leaves much to be desired."

"You've got to learn to live with it."

"But not every minute of every day. I need a safety valve."

Amy chewed a mouthful of eggs and sausages. Drank some coffee.

"Maybe we shouldn't get married," she said.

"I love you. You love me. Don't you?"

She nodded. "But we're not really in synch."

Daniel stood up, walked around the table, bent over her, put his arms around her.

"Amy, believe me: If we were too much alike, it wouldn't be any fun."

She didn't answer him. Kept chewing.

"Believe me," he repeated.

She just kept chewing.

...

Early afternoon. They walked to Central Park. Through the park. There were people everywhere, tasting the weather.

It was warm enough to sit by the Pond. They did.

A young black musician, a few yards away, was blowing the blues on a saxophone.

"When we get married, would you rather live in the city after all?" Daniel said. "There's always so much going on here."

"Too much. I can never slow down."

"Not a great place to raise kids, either."

"Right."

"You see?" he said. "We're mostly in synch."

She took his hand. "I'm sorry about what I said before. I didn't mean that. But sometimes it's as if you're sixteen years old."

He raised her hand to his lips. Kissed it.

"I know the world isn't a movie," he said. "My life with Ginnie wasn't exactly a romantic dream."

"But you were in love with her, weren't you?"

"I was."

"Why didn't it work?"

"She wasn't who I pretended she was."

Amy nodded. "She didn't try to fool you. You invented someone named Ginnie and fell in love with her. And then you were disappointed when she decided to be the real Ginnie. That wasn't her fault."

"I know."

"If we get married, Daniel, our life won't be a romantic dream, either. Nobody's life is."

"I know that."

"Do you?"

"I do. I'm going to get fat and bald. And so are you."

Amy laughed. "Fat, I can do. Bald is a stretch."

"You said, '*If* we get married.' Does it have to be *if*? Why not *when*?"

"I want to be sure. Two divorces is at least one too many."

Daniel put his arm around her shoulder. Pulled her closer to him.

"I've always loved you," he said. "You know that. I even asked you to marry me a long, long time ago. Remember?"

"No."

"We were ten years old."

"Really?"

"Really. But you weren't ready for that kind of commitment."

Amy smiled. "I'm not sure I'm ready now."

"Would a couple of glasses of wine and some Italian food get you in the mood?"

"Maybe."

"There's only one way to find out," he said.

■■■

After an early dinner, they saw *Jules and Jim.*

On the walk back to her apartment, Daniel said, "I must have seen that movie five or six times when it came out. I love it. Did you like it?"

"No."

"Why not?"

"I hate that idea—that women are mysterious. Forces of nature. That's just another excuse for not taking us seriously."

"But she was enchanting."

"She was a selfish bitch. What the hell was so enchanting about her?"

"She looked like an ancient goddess."

"Daniel, that's movie crap. She ruined their lives. She was married to Jules, but she was unfaithful to him. She didn't give a damn about their daughter. And then she killed herself and Jim. If you knew a woman like her in real life, you'd hate her guts. But in a movie, she's *enchanting.*"

Daniel didn't argue.

"I love that song," he said. "*Le Tourbillon.* It means, The Whirlwind."

"By the time we got to the song, I stopped reading the titles."

"I have the screenplay. I bought it years ago. The song is about two lovers who keep coming together and being pulled apart. Over and over again. By the whirlwind of life. *Le tourbillon de la vie.*"

"I liked the melody."

"Finally they realize that they should stay together. Because they love each other."

"Is that why you wanted me to see that movie?"

"Yes."

"I'm not a force of nature, Daniel. I'm a person."

"I love you, Amy. Will you marry me?"

She stopped walking. Looked down for a moment. Looked up at Daniel.

"Yes, I will," she said.

But it almost sounded like, Not yet.

16

Autumn

I called Mandy three, four, five times over the next couple of weeks. Tried to make a dinner date with her. Or a lunch date. Or an anytime-you're-available date.

No sale. She was in the middle of a big-money case. Had other plans. Had a touch of the flu. Was leaving the next day on a business trip.

In other words, "I'd rather not see you."

No surprise, I guess. The night of Ted's party, I had opened some old doors. Old wounds, too.

I was encouraged. If she was that anxious to avoid me, I must still matter to her. I had to find out how much I mattered.

She sent me a birthday card. A funny one. In bad taste. Along the lines of "Best wishes to an old lecher. Keep it up, even if you *can't* keep it up." Not Mandy's usual style. Or maybe it was a warning shot across the bow.

I'm not easily discouraged. I kept calling. I wore her out.

So in mid-October she agreed to meet me for a Sunday lunch in the city.

I was hoping for a balmy day. We'd stroll here and there. Reminisce. Rekindle the fire, maybe.

No such luck. It was chilly, cloudy, gray—very autumn. Which, as you know, I love. But she doesn't.

I met her in the lobby of her apartment building.

"Why don't we go to *Bonnie's?*" I suggested. An old hang-out from our salad days. "It's still in business, right?"

"Barely."

"We can go somewhere else."

"There's a new place a couple of blocks from here. On 82nd. Good food. Not too noisy."

"Lead the way."

We walked briskly, exhaling vapor clouds.

"You've been working your ass off lately," I said, pretending that I believed her excuses.

"Yes."

"So you're still not slowing down."

"I'm trying."

"And you still love what you do."

"Yes."

Short answers. As chilly as the day.

"You know, I used to think it bothered me that you were so successful," I said.

She didn't say anything.

"But that wasn't what bothered me."

Silence.

"It was how much you enjoyed your work."

"What's wrong with that?"

"I was envious. I wished I felt that way."

"Wishing has nothing to do with it. You made your choices."

"I know, I know."

"You knew that twenty years ago. Thirty years ago."

She was more comfortable now. More animated.

"I agree. I should have made other choices," I said.

"Don't blame that on me."

"It wasn't your fault."

"Absolutely not," she said, almost too softly to be heard.

She dug her hands into her coat pockets. I assumed that meant, "Discussion over."

After a minute or two, she broke the silence.

"What's going on, David?"

"I told you. I've been thinking about the past. Writing about it, too."

"*Past* means *over.*"

"Maybe it's not over."

"It is for me."

I paused. Watched our vapor clouds rise and disappear.

"How come you never wanted a divorce?" I asked.

"Why bother? It's not like I planned to get married again."

"So it was just a technicality."

"That's what marriage is. Half the young people I know don't go to the trouble. Not even when they have kids."

She stopped. We had reached the restaurant.

It was sleek, shiny, Art Nouveau.

The *maitre d'* fluttered over. He knew Mandy. Practically kissed her ass. He seated us at a quiet corner table.

The waiter appeared at my elbow. He was dressed better than I was.

"I will be your server. I am Maurice."

Our server poured coffee. We ordered lunch. I could guarantee that the portions would be small.

"I'll ask you again," Mandy said. "What's going on?"

"You make it sound so mysterious. I just want to reconnect with you."

"Reconnect? What am I, a railroad car?"

"Mandy, it's September. I've started remembering things."

"It's October."

"September. October. It's the autumn of our lives," I added, with a melodramatic flourish.

"Never mind the poetry. Memory Lane doesn't appeal to me."

"We have good things to remember."

"I suppose so."

"Our first trip to San Francisco."

"David . . . "

"What a disaster that was. Missing our plane. Getting bumped up to first class on the next flight."

"And all we had was that one *huge* carry-on bag."

"Great fun."

She smiled.

"That was a million years ago," she said.

"Or the New Year's Eve weekend we spent in Paris."

"In the rain."

"Dancing in the rain. Watching the fireworks on the Place de la Concorde."

"Yes," she said.

That was a soft *Yes*.

"The night we celebrated when you made partner."

She nodded.

"Or the morning Philip was born."

"David, please."

"What's wrong with remembering?"

Lunch arrived. An egg-white garden omelet for her. A feta cheese omelet for me. The portions were small.

I began to eat. Mandy didn't.

"What do you want from me?" she said.

"I miss being with you."

"It took you ten years to figure that out?"

"I was confused when we broke up. I didn't know what to do. What to think."

"I felt empty."

"Exactly."

"I couldn't kick that feeling," she sighed.

"We didn't have a family any more. Philip was a stranger. I didn't want to be with you any more."

"Now you do?"

"Yes, I do," I said.

"Why?"

"I told you. I miss you."

"You don't even know me any more."

"I'm not the same, either."

"Yes you are. You want to talk about all the good things. The days of our youth. New Year's Eve in Paris. Romance."

"Memories."

"What I remember is Lisa."

"She's one of the good things, isn't she?"

"I remember how she died. In pain. Afraid."

"But we had her good times, too. And we had a lot more."

Mandy picked up her fork, stood it on the table, tines down, studied it.

Suddenly less sure of myself, I confessed, "I don't know if it's going to work out."

"Maybe we shouldn't try."

"I think we should."

She leaned back in her chair. Put her fork down.

"When the alarm goes off in the morning," she said, "I hate the sound of it. You know the way I used to be. I used to charge out of bed. Let me at 'em!"

"You thought sleep was a waste of time."

"Now sleep seems very tempting."

She picked up her fork again and began to eat.

After several mouthfuls, she asked, "What's your plan? Are we sailing off to Tahiti together?"

"Not until next week."

She smiled. "That gives me some time to pack."

"I don't really have what you'd call a 'plan'. I'd just like to get together. Do things together. See how it goes."

She nodded.

"I still love to look at you," I told her.

"An old bag like me?"

"I still love you."

"Do you?"

"Yes."

"You want me to say that I love you, too. I'm not sure I do."

"It took me a year to convince you the first time," I grinned. "I'm a patient man."

Mandy played with her fork. Looked at me.

"I don't know, David. Do I miss you? Do I have anything left to give you?"

"I think you do."

"We'll see. We'll do a trial run."

"That's all I want. A trial run."

I looked around at the restaurant. "And next time we have lunch together, if it's all right with you, can we go to a place that has *waiters*, not *servers?*"

Mandy laughed, just the way she used to.

The trial run is going well, so far. We've been having fun. We hold hands. We kiss goodnight. We haven't made love yet. We will.

We may move in together again, one of these days. I think so. I hope so.

We've reached out to Philip. We've spent time with him. We're still ill at ease with him and he's still uncomfortable with us. We hope we can change that.

I gave Mandy the unfinished manuscript of my new novel.

After she read it, she had only two things to say. One: It was the best thing I'd ever written. Two: It was too close to home. And if it was published, she would never forgive me.

I argued with her for a while. Artistic integrity and all that. Then I let her win the argument. I wouldn't try to publish the book. I wouldn't even finish it.

And she forgave me anyway.